James Payn

A Prince of the Blood

Vol. II: a novel

James Payn

A Prince of the Blood
Vol. II: a novel

ISBN/EAN: 9783743420045

Manufactured in Europe, USA, Canada, Australia, Japa

Cover: Foto ©Andreas Hilbeck / pixelio.de

Manufactured and distributed by brebook publishing software (www.brebook.com)

James Payn

A Prince of the Blood

A PRINCE OF THE BLOOD.

A Novel.

BY

JAMES PAYN,

AUTHOR OF

"LOST SIR MASSINGBERD," "THE HEIR OF THE AGES,"
"BY PROXY," ETC.

IN THREE VOLUMES.
VOL. II.

London:

WARD AND DOWNEY,

12, YORK STREET, COVENT GARDEN.

1888.

CONTENTS OF VOLUME II.

A PRINCE OF THE BLOOD.

CHAPTER I.

RESCUE BAY.

RESCUE BAY, as it was presently christened by common consent, in which the ladies now found themselves, presented a very different appearance from that which it had offered to their eyes twelve hours before. Not a trace of storm was to be seen on sea or shore; the breeze, which blew from the land, only just sufficed to spread the Union Jack which had already been planted on the summit of the wooded cliff, not so much in sign of sovereignty as to attract, without loss of time, the attention of a passing vessel, if such perchance should, like their own, be ever driven from her course into those unfrequented seas. The great expanse of glittering sand was already marked out into spaces for the reception of human tenants, or for the accommodation of stores, a goodly heap of which was already piled above high water mark. Knots of men, as busy as bees, were drying powder in the sun or sitting under the shade of the rocks with which the sand was interspersed, cleaning and polishing their small arms.

It was noticeable that, notwithstanding this unusual industry, every man now and then looked up from his occupation to gaze sea-wards, where operations were going on, on which, as they well knew, depended not only their hopes of future enfranchisement, but it might be even their means of subsistence. A hasty survey of the island had already been made, which, as has been said, had been found to be uninhabited; but it still remained to be seen whether it offered any sustenance for human life. Water, indeed, it possessed in plenty, for down the centre of the cliff there fell, with leaps and bounds, a silver stream of sufficient volume to make its course visible through the sand until it reached the shore, where it emptied itself into a land-locked harbour.

The reef, in fact, on which the *Ganges* had come to grief formed a natural breakwater which, though extending to the shore in a westward direction, left on the east a sufficiently broad passage to have admitted her with safety in daylight in almost any weather; while, once under its protection, she could have anchored in company with a dozen ships of the same size, shielded even from the east wind by a projecting promontory of the land. The question now on which so much was depending, was whether the ship could be got off, in which case it could possibly be towed into harbour and repaired.

In the mean time, while the present fine weather lasted, every moment of daylight was utilized in bringing off stores, provisions, and every article which could conduce to the general comfort and convenience. For this purpose, not only the boats, but also the raft, had been despatched to the reef and was now anchored on the sheltered side of it, and with the naked eye the men could be perceived

making their way across the rocks that composed it, each with his burthen on his back,
like ants on an ant-hill.

It was a strange and stirring spectacle, and
moved the two ladies much, though in a
different manner. Edith gazed upon it with
admiration, which was not without a touch
of cynicism. Where would be the use, was
the reflection that occurred to her, of all that
industry and solicitude if the wanton wind
should rise but for an hour, or the slumberous
sea begin to yawn. To Aunt Sophia's eyes
it seemed that success must needs crown such
arduous efforts. She even ventured to picture
herself once more in England, no longer
the commonplace and conventional personage
whose *rôle* she had hitherto been content to
play, but a female Ulysses, on whose lips, as
she detailed her wanderings and adventures,
quite the best society would be eager to
hang.

The interest of this distant scene for the
moment indeed made the two new-comers
quite oblivious to the fact that Mr. Ainsworth
was waiting for them, and his breakfast, in

the foreground. He had kindled a fire on which some coffee was preparing, and spread out a little table-cloth on the sand, whereon potted meats, marmalade, and other condiments were laid, as for a picnic.

"Where on earth did you get all these dainties?" exclaimed Aunt Sophia, as she warmly shook hands with him, her spirits already elevated, rising several degrees higher at the contemplation of a feast, which the air of the place rendered as welcome as it was unexpected. "My dear Edith, there are actually eggs!"

"The two surviving fowls, like all the rest of us, have been doing their duty," returned the chaplain, as pleased with the younger lady's grateful smile as by her companion's more exuberant satisfaction. "It is to Mr. Marston that you are indebted for the sundries, and to Mr. Redmayne for the potted shrimps. Mr. Doyle contributed the marmalade, but that is not to be put to his credit, for out of two pots which he brought ashore one broke in his pocket. The captain himself supplied the coffee-pot and its contents, and your humble servant collected the sticks for the fire."

" But where, except the sticks, did it all come from, Mr. Ainsworth ? " inquired Edith. " Is it possible that you gentlemen have been ransacking the *Ganges* for our comfort, while we two sluggards were asleep ? "

" While you were taking that rest which nature demanded, let us rather say, and which your courage and conduct, permit me to add, have nobly earned, some of the officers and a boat's crew made a trial trip to our old home, and picked up what they could. They are now laying her under contributions on a much more extended scale. The necessity of it is plain enough, but it goes sorely against the grain with our poor captain. He says that it seems to him like taking the money out of the pocket of a dead friend."

" Does he think, then, there is no hope of the ship's ever being got off ? " inquired Aunt Sophia, looking up from her egg as if it were addled.

" He cannot say that for certain till he has

made a more particular survey of the wreck,"
said the chaplain evasively, at the same time
bringing a telescope to bear upon the object
in question. "He is now coming off in the
jolly-boat, I see, and will no doubt bring us
news of the matter. However it may be,
dear ladies," he added gravely, "let us remember we have very much to be thankful
for even as it is."

"That is just what Robinson Crusoe said,
or was it the parrot?" observed Aunt Sophia.
Nothing was further from her thoughts than
any disrespect to the chaplain, but the effect
of the observation was disastrous.

"In such a condition as our own, Miss
Norbury," returned Mr. Ainsworth reprov-
ingly, "believe me, that the virtue it behoves
us most to practise is that of resignation to
the will of Providence."

"No doubt, no doubt; but let us hope
that things will not come to the worst," said
Aunt Sophia naïvely.

"Never say die, while there's a shot in
the locker," observed Master Conolly, as he
disposed of a sardine neatly packed in a

layer of marmalade, between a couple of sweet biscuits. It was a contribution apposite enough to the conversation, but not on the whole calculated to allay irritation. A glance which the good chaplain happened to cast at Edith, however, put all indignation out of his mind. In that calm and unmoved face he read, as he thought, an absolute submission to the decree of Fate, and remembering what she had undergone, his heart found no room in it except for pity. A silence fell upon the little group as they watched the boat, which was bringing the judge and their sentence with it. It seemed to them that he stepped out of it with a certain slowness and dignity which—though dignity was by no means naturally wanting with him—spoke of disaster nobly faced; it might, however, be the mere sense of responsibility which their position must in any case have entailed upon him. He came towards them with firm, resolute steps, and took off his cap to his fair guests with a cheerful smile.

"I hope, Mr. Ainsworth, you have taken care that these ladies, who have been placed in your especial charge, have been well provided for?"

"Indeed," said Aunt Sophia, "we have fared most luxuriously, Captain Head. My niece and I, indeed, have no words to thank you for the consideration and kindness with which we have been treated by everybody."

"That is well, ladies. So it will be, I am confident, to the end, however long we may be fated to remain in our present quarters."

"Then—then," quavered Aunt Sophia, "you think there is no hope——"

"As regards the ship, I regret to say, a few days—a few hours, if the wind should rise—will, in my opinion, see the last of her."

"Oh, Captain Head, dear Captain Head, do you really mean that we shall never see home again?"

"We are, dear madam, as Mr. Ainsworth here will tell you better than I," said the captain gently, "in the hands of God. He will do what seems best to Him and doubtless best for us. I do not ask you to give up hope, if hope is a comfort to you, but I think it would be better for us all to face the facts.

I trust we shall all do what in us lies, like Englishmen and Englishwomen, for ourselves and one another; but in my judgment, since you ask me, I think we shall never see old England more."

At these words, which were delivered by the honest captain with a certain solemn simplicity that went home to the hearts of his hearers, Aunt Sophia covered her face with her hands and wept bitterly.

Edith instantly rose, and with a glance at the rest, which, gentle and apologetic though it was, forbade them to follow, led her agitated companion to her tent. The others stood looking at one another in consternation, as men, who are not by nature 'roughs,' are wont to do at the sight of a woman's tears.

"What a fool's trick it was of mine," murmured the captain, penitently, "to blurt out the truth like that."

"You have nothing to reproach yourself with," returned the chaplain, confidently. "It is much better that she should know the worst at once, than delude herself with false hopes."

There was an uncomfortable pause, and then the captain, lowering his voice, observed, "I was not thinking so much of the one that was working at the pumps, but of the other. Did you hear what that poor girl said when I told them that we should never see old England more? She said, 'Thank Heaven.'"

"Yes, I heard her. I don't think, however, she quite knew what she was saying."

"Driven out of her wits, eh, by my blundering speech? Well, the next time I have any bad news for her you shall break it yourself. Heaven knows I had rather go without my breakfast any day than she should have an ache in her little finger. But since the mischief's done, and the coffee's here, you may pour me out a cup, Conolly."

CHAPTER II.

THE CAPTAIN'S SPEECH.

As when a railway train is rapidly emptied of its luggage on a platform when the express is almost due behind it, so were the contents of the *Ganges* hurried over her side and into the boats. Not an hour of the calm weather, nor of daylight, was wasted; for it was well understood by all, that whatever seemed precious now would have a fancy value a few weeks hence, and might even make the difference of life or death. Though the captain's resolution as regards the vessel was acknowledged to be a sound one, there was still a hope that, after all which was necessary to their immediate existence should be got out of her, her timbers might be made use of to build another ship; but for this a long spell of fine weather was indispensable, as the con-

veyance of anything of size and weight across
the reef was very difficult, and the prognosti-
cations of the barometer were far from favourable.   For the present, however, morning
after morning dawned in sunshine and with
softest airs, and every evening saw the acqui-
sitions from the ship immensely increased.
To the more thoughtless and sanguine, it
seemed that the stores thus accumulated would
last for ever; they said to themselves with
Robinson Crusoe, that never before were shipwrecked men so well provided ; but to those
of better judgment it was plain, that unless
the island itself could be made to yield them
support, they would be in the position of men
who live upon their principal, and that a day
must needs come, and that at no distant date,
when there would be nothing left to feed so
many hungry mouths.

The investigation of the capabilities of their
place of exile were, however, for the time post-
poned for the work of salvage.   The spectacle
of so much industry amid a scene so fair was
in itself exhilarating.   If our first parents had
had some occupation in their idle hours in the

Garden of Eden, besides loafing and spooning, it is probable that they would not have made such a fiasco of matters. Even the ladies, who might easily have pleaded exemption from the common toil, put Eve to shame in this respect, for instead of roaming over their lovely dwelling-place in search of fruit, they busied themselves in sorting out whatever articles required care and good keeping, and in storing them afresh in such places as the captain deemed desirable. This employment prevented their minds from dwelling upon their respective calamities, while the invigorating, though genial, climate restored both strength and spirit.

The solicitude with which they were treated by almost all hands, had also its encouraging effect, and they often found themselves, to their own astonishment, discoursing of things around them, as though they had been the environments of ordinary life, rather than of an abnormal and exceptional position. As a rule Edith was the consoler; or rather, by avoiding all reference to their past, beguiled her companion's thoughts from it. Now and then, however, she would, as it were unawares, make some allusion to it, which revealed the sepulchre where her heart was buried. On such occasions it was the elder lady's part, not indeed to comfort her, for such a task she knew to be beyond her power, but to turn the talk to other subjects.

"I cannot help thinking, Aunt Sophia," said Edith, as the two ladies sat in their tent one evening comforting themselves with a cup of tea after the labours of the day, "that this must be one of the Enchanted Isles that sailors believed in until within the last hundred years."

"That must be before the geographical books began to be published, I suppose?"

"Not at all. I remember in that old geography of De Lisle, which dear papa used to set such store on, they were marked in a map as Basil and Asmuda. Even so late, he once told me, as 1750, an island never before known, but covered with fields and woods, and very fertile, was seen in the Atlantic, and so strongly vouched for, that ships were sent from England to explore it."

"I hope they will be sent to look for this one," sighed Aunt Sophia.

"It is hardly likely, though the parallel holds good in other respects; for De Lisle's notion was that it was the country of ghosts, and are we not here the ghosts of our former selves?"

"I must confess that we have very good appetites for ghosts," observed Aunt Sophia drily; a rejoinder, simple and commonplace though it was, far more judicious and effective than any falling in with the other's mood would have been. It had, also, the advantage of being true. In their new abode their physical health was perfect; in such a climate, indeed, there was little fear of its being otherwise, except through the monotony of their lives; and of this, as it turned out, the castaways had not long to complain.

It was the fifth evening after their disaster, and everything that could conduce to use and comfort had been taken out of the vessel. On the next morning it was understood that the much more serious work of taking her to pieces was to be commenced. The men were in excellent spirits in anticipation of this, the first step towards escape from exile, though the carpenter had reported that the bands of the ship had given signs of starting, and that it was unlikely she could hold together much longer. The ladies were still at their tea, when suddenly the boatswain's whistle sounded thrice. They knew it to be the signal for the assembly of the whole ship's company, and started up in some alarm. Though not of course included in the summons, they immediately repaired to the larger bay, and on their way were met by Master Conolly, who, foreseeing their apprehensions, had come in haste to allay them. Some trouble, he explained, had arisen with one or two of the men, who had helped themselves from one of the liquor casks, and the captain was about to address the ship's company upon the matter.

In vain the young midshipman endeavoured to persuade his fair companions to return to their tent; their curiosity was too strong to be overcome, and he could only induce them to accept his escort—a protection which, as it turned out, was not altogether superfluous.

Not one or two only, but a good many of the men, exhausted with their day's work, and urged by the natural liking which most sea-men entertain for strong liquor, had taken advantage of the accidental breaking of a cask of rum, to drink freely, and had become very noisy and elated. They gave, indeed, a mechanical obedience to the summons of the boatswain, but it was plain from their air and manner that they were in no condition to listen to the voice of authority. The majority of the crew, however, who with them had formed a ring about the captain and his officers, maintained an attitude of respectful attention. Something had already happened which was not intelligible to the new-comers, but which could be partly guessed at by the attitude of the persons concerned. Close to the captain were three sailors, Mellor, Rudge, and Murdoch, looking very flushed, and to say truth, somewhat mutinous. They had borne by no means a good character on board the *Ganges*, so that it was not surprising that they should have misconducted themselves on shore. Yet the captain not only regarded

them with such troubled and anxious looks, as
were inexplicable to all acquainted with his
resolute and dauntless character, but was addressing them in terms of consideration rather
than remonstrance. "You have had a hard
day's work and little to eat, and therefore
there is much excuse for you. But I must
say to you, as indeed I say to all, that there
is nothing more dangerous to persons in our
condition than indulgence in drink."

"That's all gammon," interrupted Murdoch
huskily; he was a huge man, beside whose
giant form, with his large arms and hairy
chest, even the captain's stalwart frame was
dwarfed; "since we are here we mean to
enjoy ourselves, and we don't mean to be
preached to neither, nor yet bully-ragged as
though we were still on board of that cursed
old hulk yonder."

"That's so," and "So says I," growled the
other two men, while a faint murmur of applause went up from a few others in different
parts of the assembly, which showed that they
were not without their sympathizers.

The majority, however, maintained a silence

which was equally significant. They seemed only less amazed at their comrades' audacity than at the patience and toleration with which it had been borne.

"I am sorry," returned the captain, in firm but quiet tones, which made themselves audible even to those who, like the ladies and their conductor, stood on the very outskirts of the crowd, "that you should so speak of the old ship which has been our home so long, and I hope, upon the whole, not an unhappy one."

"Quite right, sir," "A good home," "Ay, and with a good captain, too," went up from the now excited throng in all directions. The captain took off his cap, and the men began to cheer, but became instantly silent as he recommenced.

"I say I am sorry that any man who has sailed with me should entertain such unpleasant recollections of his voyage, or of the 'cursed old hulk' as he calls it, which we are looking on yonder, it may be, for the last time."

"We don't want no palaver; we wants to

enjoy ourselves, we wants rum," cried the mutineers, with drunken vehemence.

"Let the captain speak." "Never mind black Murdoch, sir." "Three cheers for the old *Ganges!*" replied the crowd.

"Rum is very good in its way, but we may have too much of it," observed the captain, with all the gentleness of a moralist, "and especially when, as in our case, men are cast ashore upon an unknown land, subject it may be to the attack of savages, at whose mercy our lives may be placed at any moment, and dependent for our slender chance of escape upon the efficiency and alertness of those on the watch for a passing sail. It would be hard to be deprived of all hope of seeing our own country again, with our wives and sweethearts, because some drunken scoundrel or another couldn't keep from the rum."

"That's so!" "Three cheers for our wives and little ones!" "Home, sweet Home!" "You know what's best for us, captain!"

"I think I do; but as has been proved to me pretty clearly by the conduct of one or two of you here, whom I will not name, I am no longer your captain."

"We know that fast enough, master," exclaimed Murdoch, triumphantly; "you are no master now, nor ever will be, yah!"

"Well that is a matter entirely for our own consideration, my men," continued the captain; "the most votes must carry it. It is quite true, since the *Ganges* is not a King's ship, that with the loss of her, I have lost command of *you*. You no longer owe me any obedience; but that some one to hold supreme authority must be chosen by you, is certain, if we would live here for a day, without flying at each other's throats. Fix upon whom you will, so long as he be honest and sober, but when he is once chosen let his will be law. Even what has occurred to-night shows, I think, the necessity for such an arrangement, while to-morrow—well, for all we know, to-morrow it may be too late to make it. Suppose an enemy attack us, with no one to give an order how to repulse him. Suppose a ship came in sight, and fifty men crowd into a boat where there is only space for ten, and we lose her!"

" Right, right, we'll choose *you*, captain, there's nobody but you *to* choose," came from all parts of the crowd.

" Oh, yes, there are lots of others to choose from," continued the captain smiling, "and whom you do choose must be elected in a proper manner. It won't do to shout for Jones to-day and for Smith to-morrow, and your decision, whatever it be, must be put down in writing. You will find a paper in yonder tent, with pen and ink all ready for you, and the chaplain to explain matters, and show where the mark must be put for those who are no scholars. Every one in the ship's company, officers and men, will find his name there, and every one will vote for whom he likes ; only remember this, that once recorded, it cannot be cancelled. Now go and choose your king."

CHAPTER III.

THE PLEBISCITE.

THE notion of a Plebiscite is always an attractive one to all communities.

It was true that on the present occasion the matter was generally understood to have a foregone conclusion. The majority of the men were too much attached to their old captain, and had too great confidence in him, to think of electing any one else to rule over them; but still they were flattered by the idea of choosing for themselves. They crowded into the tent with alacrity, where Mr. Ainsworth was seated at the table with 'the agreement,' as it was simply called, but on which in truth very much depended. It set forth the peculiarity of their position, and the necessity it involved of having some lawgiver and leader, against whose fiat there should be no appeal; while it left to every man the power of giving his vote to any member of the ship's company he pleased.

The proceedings were not without a certain solemnity, for those who took part in it were filled at least as much with the sense of their own importance as of that of the matter in hand; nor was the ceremony by any means a brief one.   Many of the sailors could not write, and most of them had to be separately instructed in the novel duty demanded of them; while even the most accomplished took some time, with much leaning of their heads upon one side and screwing of their courage (and their mouths) to the sticking-place to execute their autographs.   At last, however, all was done, though not before the fall of night had necessitated the use of torches in the tent, which cast their lurid glare upon a scene which was in truth eminently pictur-esque and striking.   In the open air, on the other hand, there was still light sufficient for the conclusion of the proceedings.

The chaplain presently emerged from the tent bearing the document with its long file of signatures, and, followed by the whole of the ship's company, moved towards the spot where the captain with his officers, or, rather, with those who had hitherto occupied that position on board the *Ganges*, awaited his approach. After a few words of preface, Mr. Ainsworth stated that one other person only beside their late commander had been nominated for the post of president, or leader, and as the names of those who had voted for the individual in question were but few, he suggested that it would be more convenient to read them out in the first place.

At this there was some applause, and not a little laughter of the sarcastic sort, which was instantly stilled at the sound of the captain's voice.

" If, as I understand, my men," he said, " the great majority of you have decided to replace in my hands the authority which I before possessed, it seems to me that it would be invidious, and, indeed, unfair, to those who have come to a contrary conclusion, that their names should be made public. I neither wish to know who they are, nor to know who it is

that in their judgment has appeared to them
preferable to myself. I shall take it for
granted that both he and they will acquiesce
in the decision of their shipmates, as I should
myself have done had the case been reversed;
and I hope no feeling of bitterness or disappointment will remain in the breasts of any
one of you."

The simplicity and straightforwardness of
this address went home to the hearts of its
hearers, chiefly, perhaps, because the majority
of them were themselves simple and straight-
forward. The reflection would have occurred
to a more sophisticated community that a
reference to the agreement itself would at any
time put the captain in possession of the information of which he had so chivalrously
declined to avail himself; but this idea presented itself neither to him nor them. A
round of cheers arose from the crowd as the
captain took off his cap. It was a thing he
rarely did, except at prayers, and was significant of his being about to make an important
communication. "The first act of my new
command," he said, " is to reinstate my friends

and yours" (here he pointed to the officers who stood around him, and who, by their abstinence from voting, had tacitly shown their acquiescence in the government of their chief) "in the same positions of authority which they have hitherto respectively occupied. Your vote of this evening evidently approves their re-appointment, and you will obey them, I feel sure, as cheerfully as you will obey me."

Another hearty round of cheering here greeted the speaker; his allusion to their evident wishes (though it was probable they were unconscious of having entertained them) gratified them hugely; and, moreover, with one exception, they were well satisfied with their officers.

As the captain looked round on the circle of approving faces, he perceived that enthusiasm for the new order of things had reached its acme, and that the moment had arrived for the crucial test of the obedience of his voluntary subjects. "The first order I have to give you men will, I know, be an unpopular one," he said, in a low but decisive tone; " but when I tell you that in my opinion it is absolutely necessary, not only for the maintenance of that authority you have just ratified, but for the safety of our lives, you will understand that it must be executed at once, and without a murmur. In the beautiful climate in which Providence has pleased to place us, it may be for the remainder of our days, strong drinks of any kind will be only necessary to us as a medicine. One of those liquor casks yonder will therefore be placed in the custody of Mr. Doyle. The rest you will break up at once, and in my presence."

An ominous silence ensued upon this mandate, followed by a murmur of unmistakable dissent.

" Do you hear me ? " continued the captain, in a voice at least as ominous ; it was like the growl of a lion aroused from sleep. " I must have those spirit casks broken up."

At first not a man stirred from his place ; then out from the throng marched Matthew Murdoch. The effects of liquor were still very discernible in him, though he knew, as the saying is, "what he was about;" there was less of audacity in his manner than there had been an hour ago, and he exchanged a word or two with those about him—an appeal, no doubt, for their moral support, which was presumably accorded to him—before he once more confronted the captain; his air, though impudent enough, was not so defiant as heretofore; and there was something of remonstrance, mingled with rebellion, in his husky tones.

"Look here, captain; right is right, but reason is reason——"

"Stop!" roared the captain, in a terrible voice, and looking round him with eyes from which all shrank on whom they fell. "Is this drunken dog, my men, your spokesman?" he inquired, incredulously.

Not a sound was heard save the breeze in the trees and the lapping of the sea upon the sand; then, after a pause, two replies broke forth, "Yes, he be."

"Come out and join him, then, you skulking curs."

Then Mellor and Rudge came out in a

shamefaced manner, aud ranged themselves beside their ally.

" Are there any more ? "

The wind and the sea alone made answer. The moment, it was felt by all, was a supreme one, though few pictured to themselves its immense importance; the ladies, whom it concerned most of all, the least.

Aunt Sophia, indeed, was dumb with fear; she felt that matters were in a state of tension, which could only be relieved by some act of despotic authority upon the one hand, or of lawless violence upon the other, but her alarm arose from that mere shrinking from the appeal to physical force which belongs to woman's nature; she thought neither of consequences nor of the opposing forces—the ignoble and the heroic—which composed the spectacle before her, and whose collision, like that of two thunder-clouds, was about to evoke an explosion.

For Edith, on the other hand, the scene had a dramatic interest, so powerful and absorbing that it left no room for apprehension. She had not believed that any incident of the life that was left to her could have so moved her. The reason of this, though she was unaware of the fact, was its absolute novelty. Her capacity for emotion had not, as she imagined, been destroyed; her sympathies were as quick and tender as ever, but they could no longer be approached by the old road. No by-play of the drama escaped her. She noted the attitude of the captain, a statue of wrought iron; his firm-set lips that repressed the pent-up fire within, and the eyes that betrayed it. She marked the ungainly but significant pose of the mutineer; his giant arm advanced to accentuate his words, his huge hand trembling with hate and fear and liquor, and with every now and then a glance over his shoulder, as if to make sure of the presence of his supporters.

Warned by the continued silence that speech was expected of him, he resumed his remonstrance. "Reason is reason, says I, and it stands to reason that being our own masters with plenty of leisure and victuals, that we should no longer labour but enjoy ourselves. What we men wants——"

" You mean *you* men, you three," interrupted the captain.

" Nay, it's what we *all* wants, only all have not the pluck of Matthew Murdoch to say it; we wants, since we are ashore, to taste the sweets of plenty. Now, there is nothing so sweet in life—save a lass—as good liquor; and as to destroying all them casks, I tell you straight out it shan't be done."

As he ended, he touched, perhaps by accident, or to emphasize his argument, with his projected finger his commander's arm, which instantly, as if some powerful spring had released it, struck out from the shoulder like a catapult, and levelled him on the sand. There he lay, like an ox in the shambles, and almost as huge, bleeding from the slaughterer's axe, for the other's fist had caught him in the jaw, and had knocked out a tooth or two.

" When that mutinous dog comes to himself," thundered the captain, with a look of contempt at the prostrate hulk before him, " put him in irons. And now, my men, break up those spirit casks, and be quick about it."

Both orders were obeyed without a murmur;

the irons used in punishment had, as it happened, been brought from the *Ganges*, with the other resources of civilization, and were presently fitted to Murdoch's huge form by the carpenter, who was also sergeant-at-arms; while the men, in gangs, each under an officer, proceeded at once to break in the heads of the spirit casks, and empty their contents upon the sand.

It was not one of those 'moral victories' of which so much is often made by the party which, according to the poor evidence of the senses, has unquestionably been beaten, but a substantial triumph of authority. Not until all was over was it fully understood by those most interested in the struggle (and even then only by a vague sense of relief) how doubtful had been the issue; if Murdoch had not laid his finger on the captain, the opportunity might have been wanting which had brought the "skirts of happy chance" within his grasp, but as it happened that one knock-down blow had re-established his supremacy.

Aunt Sophia had been a little shocked by

it; the appeal to brute force—notwithstanding the acknowledged admiration of the fair sex for the display of physical strength—had jarred upon her gentle nature.

"Do you not think, Edith," she said, as they returned to their tent under the young midshipman's escort, "that it would be a gracious and proper thing in us to ask the captain to pardon that poor man?"

"I am not sure," was the quiet reply. "I bear, of course, no more ill-will against him than you do, but I should like to think about it a little before joining in such a request."

"I wonder who it was that was put forward as the opposition candidate to the captain," observed Aunt Sophia, presently.

"He particularly said that he did not want to know," remarked Edith, with a half smile.

"Quite right and very proper in him, my dear," replied the elder lady; "but, then, I *do* want to know. Mr. Conolly, I see *you* know; come, tell us all about it!"

The unfortunate youth looked not a little

embarrassed; if he could have got away from Aunt Sophia he would probably have done so, and parleyed with her from a distance, but her ample arm was hooked to his. He cast a glance of distress at Edith that seemed to say, " Pray observe that it is not *my* fault; I am obliged to tell her," ere he replied to her question.

" I believe, Miss Norbury, that the other candidate for the men's suffrages was Mr. Bates. He had only a very small following; but that fellow Murdoch and the two others, Rudge and Mellor, were among them. It was in my opinion the worst choice they could have made," added the young fellow, still glancing furtively at Edith's face, which had suddenly grown very grave and pale.

" Mr. Bates is not a favourite of mine I'm sure," observed Aunt Sophia, " but we must remember, Mr. Conolly, it was not his fault that he was put in nomination. As our good captain says, let bygones be bygones; and don't you agree with me that it would be, so to speak, a pretty thing in dear Edith and myself, as well as acceptable to his friends, to get this poor man off his punishment."

Master Conolly twiddled his cap, and hesitated, with his eyes fixed interrogatively on the younger lady.

"Of course, Murdoch will be glad to avail himself of your kind intercession," he said, "but knowing the ill-conditioned set of fellows to which he belongs, I doubt whether they will like you a bit the better for it."

"Moreover," put in Edith, with sharp decision, "I was once told by one very dear to me, and who was kindness itself, that it was always a mistake to attempt to conciliate the base and cruel, since it only makes them think you are afraid of them; and as I am not afraid either of Mr. Bates or his following, any interference of mine on their behalf would produce a false impression."

It was the first time that of her own free will Edith had referred to her lost lover, even indirectly, since his death; and it was destined to be the last. Conolly, of course, understood the reason of her bitterness against Mr. Bates, but not so Aunt Sophia, who had never been made the confidant of his conduct at Simon's Bay. She only understood that her proposal for interfering with the course of justice on behalf of Matthew Murdoch had, like himself, been knocked on the head.

CHAPTER IV.

THE EXPLORATION.

To any one who doubted of the necessity of there being a supreme head to the little band of exiles, a proof was evident on the very next morning, which showed the reef without the wreck; every vestige of the unfortunate *Ganges* had disappeared, and but for the captain's urgency in getting her emptied while wind and wave permitted, many an article of comfort for which the term 'worth its weight in gold' would indeed have been an inadequate expression, would have been lost with her. Violent as must have been the storm that thus took away all trace of her, little of it was felt within the land-locked harbour, while in 'Ladies' Bay,' as the spot in which its tenants were located was called, was only heard that muffled roar

which dwellers in London associate with distant traffic, and which like a lullaby soothes
their slumbers. As Aunt Sophia and Edith
looked to seaward and saw no vestige of the
object to which they had always been wont
to first turn their eyes, they could hardly
believe the evidence of their senses. Its dis-
appearance had a very different and even
opposite effect upon them, a fact of which
both were conscious; the one was full of
regrets, the other well content with what had
happened; yet each for love's sake sympa-
thized with the other, and embraced her
without a word.

The morning, though somewhat fresher
than its forerunners had been, was fine and
bright, and the island had never looked so
beautiful. Mr. Marston called upon the ladies
early to inform them it was the captain's
orders that a more commodious residence
was that day to take the place of their tent,
and to propose that while it was being run
up, they should spend the day in exploring
their place of exile. The superintendence of
himself and his chief would be required in

getting things ship-shape and in order in the larger bay, but the services of the second mate, Mr. Redmayne, and also those of Mr. Conolly would be placed at their disposal. A couple of men would also be told off to carry their provisions, as well as to aid them in other respects; the hills into which the island was broken being very steep, and progress, by reason of the luxuriance of vegetation, by no means easy.

This proposal was accepted with alacrity. The ladies were very willing to emerge from the narrow limits of their present place of residence, and eager to explore the place that was in all probability to be their future home. A hasty survey of it, to make sure that it contained no other inhabitants but themselves, had been made on the first morning by some members of the crew, but with that exception it was virgin ground. It was quite possible that the expedition they were about to make would be the first that had been undertaken in the island, a flowery wilderness whose beauties had perhaps never before gladdened the eye of man.

To Edith the prospect afforded even a greater satisfaction than to Aunt Sophia, who remarked with some surprise the pleasure that shone in her niece's face, in welcoming their escort; she set it down to the enjoyment which she promised herself in the society of Mr. Redmayne, a very handsome and agreeable fellow. It was early days, of course, for Edith to be thinking seriously of any other man as a successor to her dead lover, but human nature was human nature, and it was only reasonable that she should appreciate the respectful and delicate attention paid her by the young officer; after all, it was only a question of time and opportunity when the widowed heart of the young girl would seek consolation elsewhere, and in no circumstances could opportunity be more favourable than in the present. So reasoned Aunt Sophia, not without a sigh, however, for the mutability of female affection, and a secret and complacent conviction that had the case been hers she would have proved more faithful, or, at all events, less precipitate in transferring her allegiance. As a matter of fact, except so far as courtesy demanded, Edith gave no thought either to Mr. Redmayne or his attentions. Her pleasure, such as it was, arose from a precisely opposite cause, namely, from the utter novelty of the situation, which prevented her thoughts from dwelling upon the love, which for her meant loss, at all, and had no sort of association with it.

Except youth and good looks Mr. Redmayne and Charles Layton had little in common ; but what similarity existed between them, so far from attracting her towards the young officer, had the reverse effect. If any comparison ever suggested itself to her mind, he suffered by the contrast. She freely acknowledged his good points, and was grateful to him for his politeness and good-will ; but to have set him side by side with her Charley would have been cruel to the one, and little short of blasphemous as regarded the other. Her position was that of an epicure, who is offered home-made Curaçoa, and who, while admitting it to be good of its kind, declines to admit the least comparison with the original.

The case of young Conolly, whom not even
Aunt Sophia could credit with any serious
intentions, was altogether different. His
society was always welcome to Edith, not on
account of his obvious devotion to her, with
which, indeed, if she had understood its depth,
she would perhaps even have been displeased,
but because he had been a favourite with
Charley. She never spoke of her lover to the
young midshipman, but her eyes often filled
with tenderness as she looked at the boy, who,
with the egotism of his age, imagined, no
doubt, that she was not wholly indifferent to
him upon his own account. The rules of
seniority had not always given him satisfaction, but on the present occasion he was well
pleased that they gave Aunt Sophia to the
custody of the second mate, and left Edith
to his particular care. In neither case was
the charge a sinecure.

The island was of small extent—not more
than twelve miles in circumference—but of
most unequal formation; except the sandy
bays that fringed it, there was hardly a level
spot to be found upon it; it consisted of

mountains and valleys, or rather of hills and dells, covered with the richest vegetation, and bright with the foliage of perpetual spring. The air which, though warm, was fresh and invigorating, was laden with the perfume of ten thousand flowers; the trees that clothed the hills themselves bore blossoms of the most brilliant hue, while the climbing plants which encircled their trunks, or which, rooted in the shelving rocks, hung in rich festoons from the edge of every precipice, gave the idea of an eternal festival of nature.

In the miniature defiles formed by the hills, this splendour of bud and bloom reached its acme; the turf, watered by clear streams, was enamelled by flowers of such bright and varied hue that as you approached it, it seemed as though you were about to tread on a carpet formed of precious stones. The blaze of colour would have been oppressive, but for the shadowy roof of the huge trees, which projected themselves on either side, and for the refreshing glimpses of the sea that were offered through their interlacing boughs.

Through this wilderness of beauty there

was, of course, no pathway; but the very
difficulty of progress enhanced its pleasure.
When a wild rose entangles our feet, it may
seem as inconvenient as a common bramble,
but the roses of this Eden had no thorns.
The creepers that hung from rock and tree
were, however, so numerous that it was impossible to escape their bonds; the wayfarers
were caught, as it were, in chaplets. On the
other hand these assisted them in their ascents
and descents; they swung themselves up and
down by ropes of flowers. Nothing that
the imagination can conceive could be more
wondrous than the spectacle of all this
lavish beauty. It kept even the midshipman
silent.

Upon the summit of the second hill, where
the Union Jack was flying, because it was the
highest point of the island, the whole party
halted as if by common consent. The view
from this spot was panoramic, and less ob-
structed than elsewhere by trees. Upon all
sides save one glittered the silver sea, without a break in its far-stretching splendour;
on the north there were two groups of islands

apparently about equi-distant from them and from one another.

"Is it possible," murmured Aunt Sophia, carried out of her ordinary plane of thought by the entrancing scene, "that our eyes are the first to behold all this?"

> "'Full many a flower is born to blush unseen,
> And waste its sweetness on the desert air,'"

remarked Mr. Redmayne, with the complacency of one who makes an apt quotation. Nevertheless it fell flat. Edith remembered Johnson's depreciatory remarks upon 'the Elegy,' and for the first time agreed with him. The situation was indeed too poetic for so didactic an illustration.

"It does not give me the notion of waste so much as of inexhaustible superabundance," she remarked.

"Just so," returned the other, with eager agreement, "and a very pleasant notion too. 'Surplusage is no error.'" To this second quotation there was no reply.

Aunt Sophia felt for Mr. Redmayne; it was clear to her that if left to carry on the conversation with Edith single-handed, it would not conduce to his interest as regarded the effacement of her former lover. She struck in therefore to the rescue. "I am not quite sure, Edie, whether the presence of these islands adds a charm to the prospect, or the reverse. What do *you* think?"

"I think that they would be better away," was the decisive reply. She did not give her reason. The fact was that they gave a vague impression of continuity, of some connection with that world without which she wished to have seen the last of, and to have done with.

"A very just expression," observed the second mate, "they would be *much* better away."

"Why so?" inquired Aunt Sophia; she knew that there was danger to her plans in drawing him out, but her curiosity was too strong for her.

"Because, though we know there are no savages on *this* island, we cannot be so sure of that as regards its neighbours."

"Good heavens!" exclaimed Aunt Sophia,

"I understood the captain to say they were uninhabited."

"He hopes and believes they are so; but time alone can show it. It is sometimes a question, with persons in our position, whether even foes are not better than no fellow-creatures at all, but that is not our case, at all events for the present."

"You mean that even foes may save us from starvation," observed Edith, "in case the island does not prove to be self-supporting?"

Mr. Redmayne nodded. The subject was evidently a serious one with him, and, indeed, it had much occupied the thoughts of the captain and his officers.

"Beg pardon, miss," said one of the sailors, breaking a rather uncomfortable silence, "but we found these pears and apples, as we come along, very, what you was pleased to call self-supporting."

"Pears and apples! You don't mean to tell me that you have been eating those great brown and red fruits," exclaimed the officer, angrily, "that hung on the trees?"

"Well, yes, sir; my mate and me we

finished up a goodish lot of them on the road,"
said the man.

"Good heavens! this may be very serious,"
muttered Mr. Redmayne, in a tone of great
concern.

"We thought they was public property,
like," explained the sailor, apologetically.

"It is not *that*, my man," observed the
officer, smiling in spite of himself; "but you
don't know what mischief you may not have
done to yourselves. One of the first tasks
Mr. Doyle has set himself to do," he added,
turning to the ladies, "is to analyze the island
fruits with a view to ascertaining their fitness
for human food."

"They are not immediately fatal to life,
sir," remarked Conolly, drily, but with an air
of great respect. "The fact is we eat half a
dozen of them apiece at mess last night."

"The deuce you did! that only shows,
however, that they do not kill midshipmen."

Despite that injurious remark, this news of
the experiment having been tried, on however vile a body, gave the speaker great
satisfaction.

"If this be so, ladies," he added, cheerfully, "then one of our gravest causes for anxiety is removed; with fruit and fish—for I take it for granted we shall find some means of catching fish—we need have at least no fear of want."

"Then, sooner or later, some one is sure to find us," put in Aunt Sophia, "that is, of course" (with a glance at those specks in the distance), "I mean some European ship."

"Let us hope so," said Mr. Redmayne gently, "though if the worst came to the worst, and we were left to one another's society for ever"—(here he blushed and stammered) —"I mean if we were exiles for life in this beautiful spot, it would not be so intolerable." He cast a glance at Edith as he ended this little speech, but she took no notice of it, and turned to the young midshipman.

"What do *you* say, Mr. Conolly?"

"I could be very happy here," he answered simply, "but I should like to see my mother again."

"A very proper reply," said Edith, with a

E 2

smile followed by a little sigh. "Come, let us go on."

A spirit of thoughtfulness, if not of gloom, had fallen upon the little party, and with a view to recover their spirits, Mr. Redmayne proposed lunch. The meal was spread in the next valley, where the sailors lit a fire, and prepared some tea for the ladies; after which refreshment, Master Conolly was called upon for a song. Our young midshipman had a beautiful voice, and sang at once 'Sweet Home' with great simplicity and sweetness. A silence followed it, more significant than any applause could have been. The rough sailors were as much touched as their superiors, and the hearts of all the audience, save one, seemed to respond with an Amen.

As they turned to leave the spot, the midshipman's quick eye lit upon a white object among the flowers, to which he called Mr. Redmayne's attention. He took it up, and examined the ground about it with great minuteness.

"What new wonder have you discovered?" inquired Aunt Sophia.

"No wonder, madam, but only a piece of information," was the grave reply. "We may now take it for granted that yonder islands are inhabited."

"Why so?"

"Because some weeks—or, perhaps, only some days—ago there has been held, close to where we are now sitting, another feast. Here are the traces of the fire, and here is a fish-bone. We must return at once, if you please, and inform the captain."

The news the excursionists brought back with them to Rescue Bay was so important that, not satisfied with their report, Captain Head himself repaired with Mr. Redmayne to the spot where the discovery had been made. That a fire had been lit there was certain, but how long ago it was difficult to guess. In a less genial climate the period might have been extended to months, but so quick was Nature to reassert herself in that marvellous region, that it might only have included as many days. Had the luncheon party been held a little later, indeed, there would have been no evidence of 'previous occupation' at all, except the fish-bone, which might itself have got there by other than human means. An osprey, for instance, might have dropped its prey. As things were, however, it was certain that there had been other visitors, and that but lately, on the island than those who at present occupied it.

"I am glad it is a *fish*-bone," said the captain, who was not without some humour. "It might have been another sort of bone, and proved our neighbours yonder to be cannibals. Even if they be cannibals, however, they will find us a tough lot," he added grimly.

"Not all of us," observed the younger officer significantly.

"Just so; there are two tender morsels you would say, one of whom might tempt even a white man. Well, well," he added kindly, perceiving the young man's look of confusion, "it's natural enough at your age that such matters should enter your thoughts, though, if you will take my advice, you will dismiss them. I know the young lady in question,

and she is not like other girls, who, having
missed their bird with one barrel, is ready to
bring down another with a second. In any
case, however, this is no time for love-making;
our island is like heaven in more respects
than one; there will be no marrying or giving
in marriage in it for some time to come. In
my judgment we shall find it a very tight
place."

"You mean we shall not be long left in
undisturbed possession of it, sir?"

The captain nodded gravely. "If the
Ganges had come ashore on the south yonder,
it is my opinion we should have seen something of our neighbours before now. As it
is, they know less of us than even we know
of them; but we may make each other's acquaintance any day."

"At all events, sir, no matter how many
they may be, we shall be able to give a good
account of them."

"No doubt, if matters should unhappily
come to that pass; but all our efforts must
be directed to keeping friends with them.
If not for our own sake, for the sake of

those whom we have in charge, and who are solely dependent upon us, it behoves us, if it be possible, to keep the peace. I look to you, Mr. Redmayne, to impress that necessity on all hands."

" It shall be done, sir."

The captain nodded approvingly; he felt not a little pleased with himself as a diplomat. One of the most difficult things in the case of a ship's crew finding themselves in native company is to keep the men from giving any cause of offence; and he felt that in what he had said to the second mate, he had offered the strongest inducement for doing his best to maintain amicable relations with their expected visitors.

CHAPTER V.

IF Mr. Redmayne alone nourished a secret passion for Edith, there was no lack of good-will and even tenderness both for her and Aunt Sophia among the rest of the castaways. They were, on the whole, good specimens of Englishmen, and, with a few brutal exceptions, understood the silent appeal made to all that was best in them, by the presence of the two defenceless women. It is possible, had the reins of authority fallen into other hands, that the responsibility of what chance had thus imposed would not have been so loyally acknowledged; but as it was, it was pleasant to note not only the delicate attentions of the officers, but the willing services of the sailors, offered on all occasions to the two ladies as though by hosts to guests.

The very first thought of the captain, as
we have seen, had been to improve their place
of residence; and in a very few hours the
carpenter and his assistants had made a dwell-
ing-house of wood, in place of the tent, but
little inferior in solidity to those scamped and
crazy edifices which the enterprising builder
now "runs up" in the suburbs of our
metropolis. Its slightness was of no consequence, for not only was the site completely
sheltered, but hardly any protection was
needed against climatic influences. It required
a fire-place only for cooking purposes, and
there were no stairs. Construction was thus
comparatively easy, but a great deal of
solicitude was expended upon its external
appearance. Not only about the ample porch
with which it was provided, but over the
whole tenement creepers were carefully trained,
which sprang up and flourished with such
marvellous rapidity that in a very short time
the hut of planks resembled a fairy bower.
Within, the arrangements were really of a
superior kind, everything that had adorned the
best cabins, including of course their own,

on board the *Ganges*, having been laid under contribution for their new abode. The sitting-room was quite handsomely furnished with mirrors, pictures, and couches, nor was anything wanting to their comfort elsewhere that forethought could supply. Aunt Sophia and Edith were far from belonging to that portion of their sex which take all kindness shown them by the other as a matter of course, or to be overpaid by a frigid smile. Their gentle hearts were touched by it.

On Edith, if such a word can be used of one so naturally sympathetic, it had a very humanizing effect; it made her feel that the terrible misfortune that had happened to her need not, as she had imagined, cut her off from her kind; the lamp of her inner life had gone out, but still she was not left in darkness; or, rather, her mental vision having got accustomed to what had seemed darkness, she became aware of a light, if of a somewhat dim and twilight kind, which struggled in to her from without. Love of the personal sort was dead within her and buried with her lost one in the deep; but sympathy with her fellow-creatures survived, and made life once more seem worth the living.

As for Aunt Sophia, whose honesty and good sense made her well aware that she had long lost those attractions which are generally associated with her sex, she had no words to express her sense of the consideration and kindness with which she was treated. " In your case, my dear Edith," she said, "it is no wonder with your youth and beauty that you should have such respect paid to you; you appear, no doubt, to this industrious hive like a queen bee, to whom it is impossible to show too much devotion; but for my part, I have nothing to recommend me but my help-lessness."

" It is that and that only, we may be sure," put in Edith quickly, " that makes these brave fellows indulge and spoil us both, as you and I would indulge and spoil a motherless child; and I wish from my heart that we had some means of showing how deeply we feel their tenderness." She thought for a moment, and then added, "I think I have hit on a plan to prove our gratitude, though it can never repay the obligation it imposes on us. It is certain, my dear Sophy, that wholesome as this climate appears to be, there will be more or less of sickness amongst us; accidents, too, it is probable will happen, even if there be not (which Heaven forbid) wounds received in active warfare with our unknown neighbours; in any case some kind of hospital will be necessary. Why should we not fit up our fourth and largest room—for which we ourselves have no real need—as a sick ward, where we may nurse our benefactors in their hour of need?"

At this Aunt Sophia clapped her hands for joy. The proposition was one which suited not only with her feelings, but her capacity, for she was a first-rate nurse. It was necessary to communicate their design to the captain, who after some demur acceded to the proposal. For some days they knew not what leisure meant, but their toil was of the pleasantest kind, since its object was the benefit of others. Under the surgeon's superintendence they selected from the ship's stores everything necessary for their purpose, and

with their own fingers pulled enough lint
to suffice for the casualties of a general
engagement.

That discovery of the fish-bone brought
indeed the curse of labour upon all the
dwellers in that isle of Eden. Not a moment
was lost in putting the encampment, if such
a term could be applied to what was no
longer a mere assemblage of tents, but which
included a wooden hut or two of some pre-
tensions, into a state of defence. A barricade
was erected between it and the sea, made by
driving a double row of strong posts into the
sand, interlaced with the branches of trees.
The space between these rows was filled with
logs of wood, stone, and sand, to render it
solid. On the inside a bank was raised, on
which the men could stand and fire if attacked,
with an opening left for one of the six-pounders
which they had contrived to bring on shore.
Two large swivels were also mounted upon
rocks, enclosed within the line of fortification,
so that they could be pointed in all directions;
and the breast-work was continued round
Ladies' Bay, right up the cliff foot.

These preparations, intended to inspire confidence, had a directly opposite effect with Aunt Sophia. She already beheld their island home invaded by countless savages, with whom scalping was a pastime, and burning their enemies alive a festive celebration. Henceforth she could never be persuaded by her companion to explore any portion of the island without an escort, and rarely even to set foot outside the barricade.

To Edith, on the contrary, this sense of impending peril was not altogether one of apprehension, and in truth had a certain charm of its own, which was due to its strangeness. Mr. Doyle, who saw much of her at this period, once remarked that Miss Edith had a passion for novelty greater than any he had observed in her sex; but the fact was that she hailed anything that was a distraction to her thoughts, even though it were anxiety itself. It is in this condition of our faculties, fortunately a rare one, that the mind is most accessible to new impressions.

One morning, as the two ladies sat in the porch, Edith with paint-brush in hand, finishing a little water-colour sketch of their rampart she had begun the day before, which Master Conolly had begged of her, and Aunt Sophia reading aloud from Walter Scott, the young midshipman came flying towards them through the passage that connected the two bays. His face was flushed with excitement more than speed, his eyes sparkled, his voice trembled with the weight of his news, as he exclaimed, "Some one has come at last!"

"Some one!" shrieked Aunt Sophia, dropping 'Quentin Durward' from her lap. "Do you mean the savages?"

He shook his head.

"Great Heaven! Is it an English ship?"

The poor lady's ecstasy was but short-lived, for the lad shook his head again.

At the same time Edith uttered a deep sigh, which he mistook for one of regret.

"I don't know what they are," he said; "come and see with your own eyes."

Edith rose at once to accompany him, and Aunt Sophia, rather than be left by herself, followed her example. As they rounded the rock, a singular spectacle presented itself.

The whole ship's company had the attitude
of a state of siege. Every man was at the
post assigned to him, on the barricade or at
the guns, with the exception of three persons
—the captain, Mr. Marston, and the Hindoo
interpreter, Gideon Ghorst—who were standing on the verge of the sea at a short distance
—for it was high tide—the first with a white
flag in his hand, the other two each with a
branch of a tree, in token of amity. The
reason for this strange demonstration was not
far to seek. In the harbour, about fifty feet
from the shore, were two large canoes kept
in a state of rest by their paddles; their
construction was most curious and graceful.
They were between thirty and forty feet long,
hollowed apparently out of a single stem.
A balance log at least twenty feet long was
carried by each at the extremity of two
immensely long elastic outriggers, the whole
presenting the appearance of excessive light-
ness and buoyancy. From stem to stern the
canoes were filled with the most gorgeous
flowers, heaped up in such profusion that
they almost concealed their tenants. These

consisted in each case of nine persons, whose appearance was so extraordinary that it was little wonder that the midshipman had been unable to classify or describe them. With the exception of one individual, who, like a native of India, wore waistcloth and turban, they were all clothed in dazzling white. Their garments, without having the stiffness of the European cut, fitted almost as closely, so as to admit of the freest use of the limbs. Their arms only, and, as was presently seen, their legs below the knee, were bare. Round their foreheads were circlets of red flowers, and also around their waists, which, contrasting with the hue of their attire, shone like crowns and zones of fire. Mr. Redmayne, who had advanced to the ladies backwards for the first time in his life, his eyes being riveted on this amazing scene, handed Aunt Sophia a field-glass.

"What do you make of them, Miss Norbury?" he inquired excitedly.

The lady's scrutiny was long and keen. "I think they are angels," presently she murmured, in awestruck tones, and passed on the glass to Edith.

If grace of form constitute an angel, Aunt Sophia's diagnosis would have been correct. So far as the assisted eye could judge of these strange visitors, they were indeed glorious specimens of humanity. Their colour was a fine bronze, no darker than that of a European who has lived long in a sultry climate; their hair was black, and very luxuriant, though so neatly arranged and confined in braids and plaits that it was difficult to judge of its length. No more feminine appearance was thereby imparted to them, however, than by the fillets worn by our street athletes; their forms—to judge by the two who were standing up and directing the rowers with their hands—were too majestic and suggestive of strength.

Had the castaways been the savages whom they had presupposed their visitors would be, they might well have imagined that those they thus beheld were gods. Astonishment, however, was by no means confined to one side. The eyes of the new-comers ranged over the encampment, the guns, and the little group of men on the shore, with the wildest surprise.

Presently the captain, raising his voice so that it could be heard by both parties, directed the interpreter to address them in Malay, which was immediately done. Thereupon the native with the turban spoke a few hurried words with the man upstanding on his canoe, and then replied, "Who are you, whom we find upon our Island of Flowers; and are you at peace with us or at war?" Then the interpreter, in obedience to the captain's orders, replied that they were unfortunate Englishmen who had lost their ship upon the reef, and that they were their friends.

On this the two leaders interchanged a word or two, and without a moment of hesitation the canoes were paddled to shore. This was done with such rapidity that the captain was unable, as it had been his intention to do, to go into the water to meet them, a sign of confidence and conciliation in such cases. He instantly, however, pressed forward, stretching out his hand to one of the leaders. The latter took it daintily in his palm, and considered it with much attention, the others crowding round with expressions of wonder and delight. They had, as their companion the Malay explained, never seen a white man before, and the blue veins in his hands were what was exciting their surprise.

The captain on this rolled up his sleeve to let them see that this speciality was not only local, whereupon they showed him their own arms, which were in their turn also peculiar, being tattooed from the wrist to the shoulder, with every description of flowers. One of the two leaders had evidently a superiority over his fellow, for which it was difficult to account; his manner was less dignified, and his curiosity and wonder more openly expressed; and on seeing the captain button his waistcoat, which happened to have come undone, he burst into a musical laugh, which was instantly echoed by the rest. His face was the most good-natured, though without weakness, it is possible to imagine, and his gentle and unsuspicious manners were those of a child. This personage, as the Malay, who could speak a little English, gave them to understand, was Masiric, brother of

King Taril, who ruled the neighbouring island.

At a word from the captain, the rest of the officers came out of the encampment to be introduced to the visitors. They naturally held out their hands, which, however, the others declined, their curiosity in that direction having been sufficiently gratified. On being informed, however, that shaking hands was a proof of friendship, they entered upon that exercise with great enthusiasm, nor could they be easily induced to leave it off. It being breakfast-time, some tea and sweet biscuits were brought down for the strangers, who partook of the beverage with seeming enjoyment; nor was it discovered till long after that they thought it the nastiest that had ever passed their lips. In every movement, look, and word, they were in short the pink of courtesy, and the most cordial relations were at once established between the two parties.

As they sat upon the ground at their repast, Edith's curiosity to get a nearer view of them induced her, in company with Mr.

Redmayne, to approach the group. No sooner did they catch sight of her than all with one accord uttered a cry of joy mingled with awe, and leaping to their feet rushed away to their canoes. From thence they presently returned, laden with flowers, and advancing towards her with every demonstration of respect, heaped them up at her feet, and then prostrated themselves on the sand.

"What shall I say to them?" she inquired eagerly of the interpreter. "What is it they take me for?"

"They worship flowers," explained the Malay, "and they take you for their goddess."

"And a very natural error to fall into, too," said Mr. Redmayne, under his breath.

CHAPTER VI.

It falls to the lot of very few of us to be worshipped even metaphorically; and Edith Norbury's position seemed to her a sufficiently embarrassing one ; but the fact was that under the circumstances she could hardly have gone wrong in whatever she did. Persons of the blood royal find it very easy to satisfy the requirements of their 'obedient humble servants,' and a Divinity has of course still less difficulty in such matters. It was natural to Edith to smile and look pleasant, and in so doing she fulfilled all that was expected of her. Moreover, as it so happened, these good people were in the most admirable cue for unquestioning devotion. Deep hid in the Isle of Flowers, which it seemed was its native designation, was a rude altar, to which at certain seasons, of which this was one, these children of nature came to pay their vows. Their offerings they had brought with them, and finding, as they imagined, the goddess in person to receive them, it seemed superfluous to seek her shrine. The situation had that sort of sublimity about it which is only one step removed from the ridiculous; had Edith been a man, for example, and one of the captain's build, his appearance with so much floral decoration would have suggested to the irreverent and European mind a Jack-in-the-green; as it was, being a woman, and a very pretty one, she seemed, as she stood knee-deep in bud and blossom, even to her own countrymen, as at least a charming Queen of the May, and their evident admiration assisted the impression produced upon the visitors.

Even Mr. Bates was pleased, because, as he explained to one of his henchmen, if these people didn't know a girl from a goddess, it was plain that they must be simple indeed, and that if the young woman only played her cards decently well she could get anything she wanted out of them, which would be to the benefit of the whole community. That she should hesitate to take advantage of their ignorance never entered into his mind, and indeed for the present it was difficult, and, as the Malay suggested, would be exceedingly injudicious, to do otherwise. Edith herself was tortured with scruples ; the position thus involuntarily thrust upon her was not only like that of the Lady of Burleigh, "the burthen of an honour to which she was not born," and for which she felt wholly unfitted, but seemed also to savour of impiety. Aunt Sophia, however, joined with the captain in advising her at least to be silent. Perhaps she felt a secret pride in finding so near a relative promoted, though by mistake, to such an immense elevation, while at the same time she experienced a little natural jealousy at having no share of these celestial honours. "They will very soon find out, my dear Edith, without your telling them, that you are no goddess," was her naïve reply to her niece's scruples. At this Edith smiled—dispensed, as it seemed to them, one more ray to her enraptured worshippers—and withdrew as 'divinely' as she could to Ladies'

Bay, followed by Master Conolly laden with her floral tributes ; just as some prima donna, who on returning from a scene in which she has been overwhelmed by public favour, is obliged to call in assistance to carry her bouquets.

While the visitors were being shown over the encampment, every object of which awakened in them a new world of thought, the Malay in the intervals of interpretation told the captain what he knew of their new friends. He himself—according to his own account, one of the best and most trustworthy of mankind—had met, as good men do, with great misfortunes. On a voyage from Canton to Amboyna his vessel had been driven far out of her course, and been ten months ago wrecked on the neighbouring island, which was called Breda. Not a soul had been saved except himself; but the people had proved very kind to him, as no doubt they would prove to the captain and his crew. So far, however, from being effeminate, as they might appear, the natives of Breda were a very powerful and warlike race, which they had need to be, since on its sister island, Amrac, there dwelt a savage and cruel people, with whom they were always at war. The island on which they now were, named Faybur (or Isle of Flowers), unclaimed by either and common to both, was seldom visited by the inhabitants of Breda, except, as on the present occasion, for devotional purposes, and by those of Amrac (who worshipped nothing) still more rarely. As to the possibilities of rescue, it was the Malay's opinion that the *Ganges* was the first European ship that had ever sailed these seas. On Faybur he had been given to understand that there were no trees fit for the construction of canoes, much more of any larger vessel; and even in Breda the timber, though extraordinarily light and buoyant, was of a very perishable nature.

This news had some satisfaction, but more of discouragement in it. It was probable that, from their present visitors and their friends, no evil was to be apprehended; but there was no knowing what changes might arise from their common enemies on the other island; while it seemed only too likely that where

they were there they must be content to
remain for the rest of their natural lives. The
captain himself had no family ties, nor was
his mind much given to sentiment; but this
decree (for such it must needs prove, if the
information of the Malay was correct) of perpetual separation from all that was familiar
affected him not a little. He felt, too—for
his heart was kind—for those of his people
who had wives and children, whose faces they
were never to see more, and whose homes
would be worse than desolate, because haunted
by false hopes of their return. His pity was
especially claimed by the two women (so unfitted by their bringing up to face such a
calamity), whom Fate had committed to his
charge, and for whose future, so full of peril,
he had become responsible. To make arrangements beyond the passing hour for them was
impossible; truly, indeed, could it be said of
them that they could not know what a day
might bring forth. Not even the present
could be relied upon, since for the captain—
who had the prejudices, or perhaps it would
be fairer to say the experience of his class—

the very name of Malay was a symbol of bad faith. He had to take his description of the state of affairs for granted, not because he trusted in the man's word, but because there was no evidence to be procured from any other source.

A circumstance at this moment occurred, which, to say the least of it, did not tend to increase his confidence in the go-between in question. The captain had besought him, in a few earnest words, on introducing the new arrivals into the camp, to say nothing of the nature of its armament ; to keep their visitors in ignorance of the existence of that last resource of civilization—powder and shot—was of the utmost importance ; and everything connected with fire-arms had been carefully put out of sight except the cannon, which could not be well disposed of, but whose presence could easily be explained to such simple inquirers on the ground of decoration. Where all was novel, a brace of swivels and another of six-pounders would excite neither more nor less of curiosity than other objects the uses of which would be equally unintelligible to them ;

and so, indeed, it had turned out. The
visitors had made the circuit of the camp, and
gorged with undigested information as any
young gentleman who goes up for a com-
petitive examination at Burlington House,
were about, with many signs of friendly satisfaction, to return to their canoe, when one of
them discovered upon the sand a bullet. This
object, carelessly dropped and as carelessly left
where it fell, or perhaps too small to attract
an eye less keen than that of a savage, at once
riveted his attention. The weight of it as
contrasted with its minuteness awakened his
wonder, and he instantly turned to the Malay
for a solution of the phenomenon. The explanation was short and swift, and seemed
sufficient, for the native pushed his inquiries
no farther; but, on the other hand, he hid the
bullet in his robe, as the captain shrewdly suspected, for further investigation and inquiry.
The Malay, had he chosen to do so, might have
put an end to all discussion on the matter, by
affecting to treat it as of no importance, and
returning the bullet to its proper owner, or
even throwing it into the sea. It was evident

he had wits and presence of mind enough to have adopted this course, had he been so inclined; and the fact that he had not done so was full of sinister significance. The possession of this little object would give him the key to a secret which he would have been otherwise unable to render intelligible to his companions. To reproach him with any such design was, however, out of the question; not to quarrel with him, and through him to conciliate the others as much as possible, was the only course open to the castaways.

It was, then, with a heavy heart that the captain saw his visitors about to depart. On the one hand, it was a matter of great convenience, and one which did away with much necessary misconception, that an interpreter between the two parties had been found; on the other, it placed in what might prove to be unworthy, or even hostile hands, a vast and irresponsible power. It was to be hoped, indeed, of a people apparently so genial and good-natured, that they would draw favourable conclusions for themselves of their new neighbours, but it was certain that their judgment was liable to be warped and perverted by the only personage who was in a position to speak with knowledge, and whose interests might prompt him to misrepresentation.

A present of some kind was given to each visitor, nor was the Malay himself forgotten. Indeed, the captain showed no little diplomacy in giving him one of precisely the same kind that was assigned to Prince Masiric, by which he wished not only to please its recipient but to arouse some jealousy in the breast of his Royal Highness. Gifts, too, of various kinds were forwarded to King Taril—a present of tea (which his Majesty, as it was afterwards discovered, took in pinches raw, in preference to the usual decoction), a jar of sugar-candy, a pound of the sweet biscuits which had given such pleasure to his subjects, and several yards of scarlet cloth.

Laden with these treasures, and delighted with their amazing experiences, the visitors were stepping into their vessels, when from the Ladies' Bay the voice of Master Conolly singing a Scotch song was borne upon the evening breeze. The effect upon his native audience was most remarkable. No exclamation of pleasure broke as before from their lips, but "the hushed amaze of hand and eye" testified to their delight and wonder. Then, with ineffable softness, so as not to interrupt the strain, the word "Deltis" passed from one to the other. The captain would have inquired of the Malay what this meant, but Masiric held up his finger for silence. A strange picture, indeed, in that exquisite frame of Nature's handiwork, was this band of enraptured savages, listening as though to a voice from heaven (and in truth it lacked neither sweetness nor pathos) to the song of the unseen lad :—

"Hame, hame, hame, oh, hame fain wad I be,
　Oh, hame, hame, hame to my ain countrie!
　When the flower is in the bud, and the leaf is on the
　　tree,
　The lark shall sing me hame to my ain countrie!
　Hame, hame, hame, oh, hame fain would I be,
　Oh, hame, hame, hame to my ain countrie!"

CHAPTER VII.

A VOLUNTARY EXIT.

Not till the song had ceased did the attention of the visitors relax for one instant, and with its last note an answering thrill seemed to pervade their giant frames. In Breda, explained the Malay, singing was utterly unknown; nor did even any bird sing, save one they called the Deltis, which had a flute-like note, not unlike that of the young midshipman, and which, visiting them only at rare intervals, was held in a manner sacred. Masiric could not be persuaded that what he had heard was a melody produced by the human voice, so the captain ordered Conolly to be sent for, to give in their presence another specimen of his powers. As a rule, midshipmen are not shy, and fortunately he was no exception to the rule, or the task

might well have proved embarrassing. Moreover, not knowing what a sensation he had
made already, he had no idea how much was
expected of him. But whether by accident
or design, he selected a song of a very different
kind from its predecessor, 'Scots wha hae wi'
Wallace bled,' which he gave with a great
deal of vigour and feeling. The effect was
even more striking than that of his previous
effort, for the visitors, as if roused to frenzy
by the stirring strains, flew to their canoes,
and snatching from them each a club—
weapons they had hitherto kept concealed—
performed a sort of war dance in rhythmic
measure. A more complete triumph was
never achieved by singer; nor, on the other
hand, did ever success exact so severe a penalty.

There was a hurried conversation with the
Malay, and then, on behalf of the visitors, he
besought, as the greatest favour and strongest
mark of friendship that could be shown them,
that the young midshipman should be allowed
to accompany them to Breda. The captain
stood irresolute; there might be great advantage in such an arrangement for the ship's

company, but there was also danger to the
envoy. "He shall not go unless he wishes it
himself," was the resolution arrived at, as he
watched the colour come and go in the young
fellow's cheek. Then he took him aside and
spoke with him. "If you shrink from this
undertaking, as well you may, my lad," he
said kindly, "do not hesitate to say so; it
may, no doubt, be of great benefit to us, if
by your singing you please the king as you
have pleased his people; but there is much
risk in it, and you have a mother at home to
whom I am accountable for your safety, and
of whom it behoves us both to think."

"I will go, sir; but I should like to wish
good-bye first to Miss Edith Norbury," was
the lad's simple reply.

Under other circumstances, such a request
would certainly have provoked some ridicule
from one so little given to sentiment as his
commander, in whose eyes Master Lewis
Conolly did not seem to have long emerged
from the nursery. As things were, however,
and considering the nature of the venture the
boy was willing to make, his very youth gave

seriousness to his appeal. As the captain was about to give him the desired permission, Edith herself made her appearance from Ladies' Bay. The news had already reached her of what had been proposed, and in an agony of apprehension for the lad's safety, she had determined—reluctant as she was to interfere with the dispositions of authority—to make her protest.

Her presence, as it happened, was welcome neither to her *protégé* nor to the captain. The former would have fain made his farewell out of sight of prying eyes; the latter was chagrined that she should have thus run the risk of cheapening herself by a second appearance before those on whom she had made so marvellous an impression. The mischief, however, if mischief it were, was done. With rapid step, flushed cheek, and eager eye, Edith came down to the shore, and as she did so, the visitors, as before, prostrated themselves on the sand. Of them she took no notice (an undesigned piece of diplomacy which probably increased her reputation with them), but addressed herself at once to the captain.

" Is it possible, Captain Head, that you are about to send this fatherless boy among a strange and it may be a barbarous people, without a single friend, or the means of making one, on the possible chance of benefit to those he leaves behind him? Let two of them—for I am speaking for my relative as well as for myself—the two on whom if evil falls will suffer the most from it, entreat of you to make no such sacrifice of a brave boy for our poor sakes; we are women, but we are not such cowards as to wish to be saved from danger at that cost." She spoke with exceeding earnestness and passion; her theme not only elevated her usual style, but seemed to inspire her very frame with a dignity hitherto unknown to it. The visitors uttered a low cry of awe and deprecation at the sight of the ire of their goddess.

"Madam," replied the captain quietly, "you do me wrong. This boy, as he will tell you, has received no orders from me to comply with our visitors' request. On the contrary, I have reminded him that he has a mother at home who, should we ever, God willing,

return to our native land, will ask me, 'Where
is my son?' and woe be to me if I have to
answer, 'His blood is on my hands.' But if
he himself is willing——"

"Oh, shame upon you!" interrupted the
girl with vehemence; "you mean if he himself is brave enough to lose his young life
for our sakes, why should we hesitate to
take advantage of so much simplicity and
courage?"

The captain bit his lips and was silent.

He was one of those men whose nature,
invincible by fire and sword, shrinks from
the sharpness of a woman's tongue.

"The captain is quite right, Miss Edith,"
said the young midshipman softly; "he has
placed no compulsion on me of any kind; but
he has offered me an opportunity of distin-
guishing myself, such as falls to the lot of
few men of my age"—it was with difficulty
Edith here repressed a smile, in which, however, it would have been cruel indeed to have
indulged—"and I am fully resolved to em-
brace it; I shall come back again, safe and
sound, no doubt, but if I do not, you will

think of me as having done my duty, and—and—not forget me."

The tears rushed to Edith's eyes, but remembering in whose presence she stood, and how important it was that she should exhibit no sign of weakness, she restrained them. She turned to the captain with an interrogating glance, but he shook his head. " I will say neither yes nor no, madam, in this matter; it never was one of discipline or duty, and I wash my hands of it. You must just settle it your own way."

" The wind is rising," said the Malay impatiently to Gideon Ghorst, " and our canoes are unfitted for rough weather; we are anxious to be off, and my people here hope that nothing has occurred to prevent the fulfilment of your promise as regards this young gentleman."

As he spoke, he threw at Conolly a glance of unmistakable disfavour, which did not escape the captain's attention. " There has been no promise," he answered coldly, when this speech was translated to him. " Now, madam, it is for you to decide."

There is nothing so popular with the crowd as an occasional self-abnegation of authority, and this deference on the part of their chief to Edith's opinion was extremely well received by the ship's company. They quite understood the affair to be one out of the ordinary course, and to be settled by no ordinary rules. As for the visitors, Edith's decision had only to be explained to them to be unhesitatingly accepted as law.

"The issue, Captain Head, which you have placed in my feeble hands," she answered modestly, but in tones so distinct that all around her could hear, "is, I feel, far too momentous for them to deal with. I do not, however, shrink from the responsibility you have imposed upon me. Let Mr. Conolly go, since he wishes it; but not utterly friendless, or without the means of communicating with his fellow-countrymen. Let our own interpreter be his companion; as he is the only medium of intercourse between us and our neighbours, they will prize him for their own sakes; and since whenever they visit us they must needs bring him with them, we shall always learn how our young envoy fares." This proposal was received by the whole ship's company with three ringing cheers, for while it possessed all the advantages for which they hoped for themselves, it mitigated the circumstances of the volunteer exile, whose youth appealed to every heart, and for whom almost every one felt both gratitude and pity.

To the Malay, however, the suggestion was very far from welcome. "The canoes are light," he murmured in broken English, "and already overladen."

"Our men need not go in the same canoe," returned the captain drily, "so no more risk will be run by one than the other. You will take both men or none—that is my last word."

Some discussion followed between the Malay and his friends, whom he was obviously endeavouring to win over to his own views; but it was put an end to by the presence of mind of Edith, who, addressing the Prince Masiric by his own name (a circumstance which caused his royal knees to knock together), pointed with outstretched finger first to the midshipman and then to the interpreter,

a gesture that was instantly understood and
its command complied with. In less than a
minute the whole party, with its two addi-
tions, were afloat, and the canoes began to
glide with amazing swiftness towards the
harbour-mouth. The young midshipman was
in the second of them, and kept his eye fixed
upon the "lessening shore" with pathetic
persistence. He was hardly more than a
child in years, and such a parting would have
been a sufficiently trying one to even the
most seasoned sailor; indeed, there were others
beside Edith and Aunt Sophia to whose eyes
tears forced their way as they beheld the last
of him, but the lad himself betrayed no
symptom of weakness. When the full-voiced
adieu involuntarily arose from the shore, con-
veying the good wishes of those he was
probably about to leave for ever, he had even
the spirit to reply to it in a characteristic
manner by singing a verse from 'The Farewell to Ayrshire':—

> " Friends, that parting tear reserve it,
>   Though 'tis doubly dear to me ;
> Could I think I did deserve it
>   How much happier should I be "—

an appropriate reply enough to the general voice, but the song was a favourite one with Edith, and it is possible that it was intended to have a meaning for her private ear.

"It is like sending forth the dove from the ark, which always struck me as a cruel experiment," sobbed Aunt Sophia.

"Let us hope, madam, that like the dove he will come back with the olive branch," said the captain cheerfully; but his rough and weather-beaten face, like that of many a one beside him, was full of tenderness and sorrow. As to Edith, she had no heart to speak, but wept in silence.

The harmony of human nature, however, is never universal, but has always some hitch or jar in it.

"I hope we've seen the last of *that* young whipper-snapper," was Mr. Bates's observation to his henchman, Matthew Murdoch, as the canoes rounded the headland. "As he's so young and tender, I shouldn't be a bit surprised if the savages boiled and eat him."

CHAPTER VIII.

THE COPPER KETTLE.

Days and weeks went by without any news of the young midshipman, or any second visit from those to whom he had so courageously intrusted himself. This silence, though very distressing to those who mourned his loss, and reproached themselves for having taken advantage of his chivalrous offer, was, however, explicable from natural causes. Of course, it might be that the intention of their neighbours had been misunderstood, and their pretended friendship only one of those cunning devices which savages often put into practice, sometimes to carry out some cruel design, but more often without any other aim beyond that of gratifying their taste for duplicity; but the idea of their having played so treacherous a part did not commend itself to the sober judgment of the captain, though it excited the apprehensions of the ladies. But while almost convinced that the lad stood in no peril from the hands of his unknown hosts, he had more serious doubts than he cared to express as to whether he had ever reached them. The storm, which the Malay had predicted, must have come up before the frail canoes, swift as they were, could possibly have got home, and they were quite unfitted to live in a heavy sea. On the other hand, if they had survived the passage there was reason enough in the rough weather that had since prevailed to account for their not having again attempted it. Though the castaways thought nothing of it, and the waters of the harbour, protected by the coral reef, remained almost unruffled, there was wild work on the sea; and what the sea could do in those latitudes the crew of the sunk *Ganges* had good reason to know.

Every day from the look-out station Edith Norbury gazed with anxious eyes upon the island, looking through the misty foam more vague than ever, but which had now so strong a personal interest for her; but she gazed in vain. Distressing, however, as were her fears for the safety of the boy envoy, they in some measure usurped the place of her former woe, and were preferable to it inasmuch as they admitted of a solution. She was never tired of talking of the lad, and of his heroic self-sacrifice, and in the hopes of his return seemed to find that tie to life which had hitherto been wanting to her. Under other circumstances, the significance of this change would not have escaped her companion's observation, nor, indeed, did it altogether do so, since in after days she often recalled the impression it had produced, but for the present Aunt Sophia's mind was too .much occupied with material matters to concern itself with psychological observation.

The preparations for the defence of the camp were pushed on unceasingly; sentries were posted day and night; there was constant practice with small arms, though no powder was expended, and all these indications of impending strife filled her with alarm. How Edith could range the island as she did without an escort was amazing to Aunt Sophia;

nor could she be made to understand that the rough weather which prevented the inhabitants of Breda from repeating their visit, must equally preclude any hostile manifestations from Amrac. Moreover, though she had had no official information of the matter, she was conscious that there were troubles in the camp itself, which her fears easily magnified into acts of mutiny. There had been meetings of the officers, and whisperings among the men, and though there was no manifestation of discontent, there was evidently a chord amiss in the general harmony that had hitherto prevailed. The truth was that there had been more than one case of drunkenness in the camp, an offence under other circumstances trivial enough, but which as matters stood was of the greatest importance.

For the question involved not only theft, but what was even a more serious crime, since it implied a guilty knowledge shared by many — fraudulent concealment. Either the strong liquor in charge of the doctor had been stolen, or the destruction of the liquor casks had not been so complete as was supposed. The latter alternative was the more probable, since no liquor was missed from the store, while the drunkenness—though limited at present to some half-dozen cases—went on almost unceasingly. In every case the culprits denied that they were guilty, and instanced the impossibility of their getting drunk as proof of their innocence. This was hard to get over, and though the captain was not the sort of man to accept the explanation of 'atmospheric influence' advanced under such circumstances by the accused, he was sorely puzzled how to act. The very plea disturbed him not a little; for it was not such an excuse as would occur to the ordinary sailor's mind. It seemed to point to some ruling and superior spirit behind the offenders. The crime itself, too, was in their position of the most dangerous kind, and might lead at once to mutiny and ruin. In the mean time, he kept these things as much as possible from the ladies' ears.

One morning, after Edith had paid her usual visit to the look-out station, she was tempted by the loveliness of the day to extend her ramble. The weather, indeed, on the island was almost invariably clear and fine, but for the first time for weeks the disturbance of the sea showed signs of abatement; the clouds to the northward were lifting, and once more revealed the island which formed the subject of so much interested speculation to her. Even in the bays it was now possible to find shelter, and descending from the higher ground, she took her way along them in contemplative mood. Headland after headland was thus rounded, without her taking particular note of anything, but drinking in the freshness and beauty of the varied scene with unconscious pleasure. In this way, without knowing it, she had made half the circuit of the little territory, and was only made conscious of the fact by perceiving that she was receding from and turning her back upon the neighbouring island. Having got so far she resolved to complete the round and return to the camp, as she had not hitherto done, the other way, when a circumstance occurred of which she thought little at the time, but which had its results.

Behind a projecting cliff there lay one of those defiles, filled with brightness and colour from a thousand flowers—though the sun was absent from it—of which the island possessed so many. She was wondering whether it might prove a short cut to the camp, when she perceived a thin line of smoke wavering among the trees. It startled but did not alarm her. It could only proceed of course from some fire kindled by members of the camp, and it struck her that she would inquire of them whether there were any difficulties in the unknown route she was about to take. As she turned up the chine, as it would have been called had it been upon the English sea-coast, she suddenly came upon a little hollow in which half a dozen men were seated round a huge copper kettle. At her approach they all jumped up with a quickness that seemed suggestive of something more than mere respect, and one of them came forward to meet her. It was Matthew Murdoch, the man who had been placed in irons on the appointment of the captain to his command. His look was angry and even menacing, and he stood between her and the rest, with his great arms akimbo, as if to stop the way.

"I am sorry to have disturbed you," she said gently, "but I have walked farther than I intended, and thought this might be a nearer way home than that by which I have come."

"Well, it isn't; it's a longer way; and let me tell you a very dangerous one," was the gruff reply.

"A very dangerous one?"

"He means precipices and that, miss," explained another sailor, stepping forward.

"No, he doesn't," growled Murdoch, "he means what he says, and she'll find it out if she comes much farther."

"Tush, tush," exclaimed the other man, "you mustn't mind him, miss; but indeed it's not a safe road to those who don't know it; and you had better go back as you came."

Edith thanked him in her usual quiet tones, and at once began to retrace her steps. Once only she ventured to look back, and beheld both the men standing together where she had left them, with the blue smoke rising over

their heads. She had, as she supposed, interrupted some outdoor festivity, and thereby
incurred the wrath of the under-bred fellow.
There was no harm done after all, nor did
she nourish any resentment against him, but
this unaccustomed roughness of treatment distressed her. With the men in general she
had always been popular, and though the
sullen behaviour of one or two had not escaped
her notice, she had set it down to a natural
moroseness of character; but in this man
there had been evidently intentional rudeness,
and she could not help reflecting, in the unhappy circumstances in which Aunt Sophia
and herself were placed, how much they owed
to the influence of authority, and how power-
less they would be without it to shield themselves from insult. Never before did she
feel so keenly the want of what is termed 'a
natural protector,' one bound by the ties of
blood or otherwise, to make her quarrel his
own. To the captain and his officers she was
conscious of being under a hundred obligations,
for which she had not been ungrateful; but it
had never before been borne in upon her, how

entirely dependent upon them were Aunt
Sophia and herself, even for those rights which
in less exceptional communities are common
and assured to all. It was a reflection she
did not dwell upon, and which in a few
minutes lost its edge, but having once entered
her mind it remained there, and, though
perhaps unconsciously to herself, had no doubt
a material effect upon her subsequent course
of conduct.

Though well resolved to make no complaint
of the manner in which she had been treated,
albeit it had had in truth more of indignity, if
not of insult, in it than can be gathered by
mere description, the incident itself had made
so strong an impression upon her that she related it, with reservation, to Aunt Sophia, who
in her turn related it to Mr. Marston.

"Your aunt tells me you had an adventure
this morning," he observed to Edith, when he
met her later in the day.

"Indeed it was not worth repeating," she
said hurriedly, lest some imprudence of his
informant should get any of the people into
trouble. "It was only that I came upon some

of your sailors making tea, who were so good as to warn me not to come home by a new way, as I had intended, and whereby I might have come to harm."

"And where was it they were when you came upon them?"

Edith described the place as well as she could, eulogized their choice of a locality for their picnic at once so beautiful and so secluded, and, dimly conscious of mischief, endeavoured to make matters as pleasant and innocent as she could.

"And how do you know, Miss Edith, that the men were making tea?"

"Well, I don't know it," she answered smiling; "they did not offer me any, it is true; but as they had a fire lit, and a large kettle upon it, I concluded as much."

"And no doubt you are right," returned the officer carelessly. "Only it seemed strange that they should have troubled themselves to take their kettle so far from home."

The explanation allayed Edith's suspicions for the moment, but before nightfall a rumour from the camp reached her ears which filled

her with consternation. It was said that in
some secret spot on the farthest extremity of
the island, the authorities had discovered certain implements, including a copper boiler and
a coil of metal, technically called the worm,
used in distillation, and that the same had
been employed in extracting from the Ti-root
(or, as Mr. Doyle more scientifically termed it,
Dracæna terminalis) an ardent spirit. Here,
then, was the mystery explained of those late
cases of intoxication which had so puzzled and
alarmed the authorities, and Edith Norbury
had been the innocent cause of its solution.
The tea party, which she had been so unfortunate as to interrupt, had been in fact a private
still.

CHAPTER IX.

ONE morning the ladies were startled at their breakfast hour by most unusual sounds: the boatswain's whistle followed by a hum of voices and a confused uproar such as is audible in the movement of any large number of persons, even on sand. There was also a sort of hollow murmur, as though a band of horn-blowers were practising on their instruments for the first time. This latter noise continued after the others had ceased. The rampart that ran round their bay, instead of its solitary sentinel, was now lined with men, who, however, had placed themselves out of sight of the sea. It seemed only too likely that the long-expected visit from their neighbours had taken the form of an invasion.

While they sat in doubt, eager to know

what had occurred, but waiting for orders from
the captain, who had bidden them in any such
case to remain indoors till he should send
them word what to do, an emissary arrived
from him in the person of Mr. Redmayne.
His Majesty of Breda, he said, had arrived, and
was about to land. He had only brought five
canoes with him, but a man from the look-out
station had brought word that a large fleet
filled with armed men was in waiting on the
further side of the island. It was possible
that Edith's presence might prove of service,
but the matter was left entirely to her own
discretion. She announced herself at once as
ready to go, and accompanied by Aunt Sophia
and the second mate, she at once repaired to
Rescue Bay.

The spectacle that presented itself was even
more striking than on the last occasion. From
where the ladies stood they could see the
whole camp in a posture of defence, although,
beheld from without, its appearance was as
peaceful as usual. The men were lying down
in the batteries, and not a musket-barrel
peeped above the parapet. The king's canoe,

which was of great size, with a raised platform in the centre, was coming up the harbour, with two others on each side of it, the occupants of which splashed the water with their paddles, and flourished them above their heads in a graceful and dexterous fashion, while at the same time they sounded conch shells, like mermen in attendance upon their sea-king.

On the platform were two persons—one a little over middle age, of colossal size, with a dignified expression of countenance, and the other a much younger man, of slighter build, and with a face so bright and eager, and yet, withal, so gentle that it might have belonged to a child. The absence of beard and whiskers increased this appearance of youth, so that until he rose and displayed his figure, which was almost as tall as that of his companion, and magnificently proportioned, it would have been difficult to guess his age, which was, in fact, nearly twenty-six. His hair was glossy black, and had a natural wave in it, equally removed from the crisp curl of the negro and the straight hair common to so many tribes of the Indian Archipelago.

Despite the alarm which the situation inspired in Aunt Sophia's bosom, her eye could not rest on so splendid an example of man's outward beauty without approval.

"Did you ever see such a magnificent young fellow?" she whispered in Edith's ear. "He looks like the bronze Apollo that used to stand in your poor uncle's library."

But Edith's attention was fixed on even a more attractive object, of which she had just caught sight—namely, the missing midshipman, who, hitherto obscured by the raised platform, could now be seen waving his handkerchief from the same canoe, in which the two interpreters were also seated.

"Look, look, there is Mr. Conolly!" she exclaimed excitedly.

"The dear, dear boy!" cried Aunt Sophia. "How glad I am!" and the tears stood in the eyes of both women.

At a word from the king, two men from the other canoes leapt into the water, and made signs to the captain that he should suffer himself to be carried in their arms to the royal barge. Such a mode of locomotion—though it is called by our children 'king coach'—is not very dignified, but on understanding that its object was to place him on the same platform as the king, thereby implying an equally exalted rank, he consented very readily. Then his Majesty with much complacency, like one who is exercising a new accomplishment, shook hands with the captain, and introduced him to his son, Prince Tarilam. The latter, to the astonishment of the captain, not only shook hands with him, but in very musical broken English observed, "Good morning, sir," whereat his Majesty clapped his hands triumphantly, and gazed upon his offspring with affectionate amazement, like a father who, while recognizing the genius of his son, admits with modesty that it is not hereditary.

It must not, however, be concluded that King Taril was deficient in intelligence. No sooner had the procession come ashore than he beckoned Prince Masiric, and bade him point out to him those objects of interest, the description of which had already inflamed his curiosity. The difference between the natures of these royal brothers was as distinct as any to be observed in the most civilized communities. They were equally observant, but the one, like the men of Athens, was captivated by mere novelty, and seemed to have little sense of comparison, while the other strove to appraise the relative value of the different objects brought to his notice with reference to their use and advantage.

In after days Edith used to liken King Taril to Peter the Great, whom, save in stature, he indeed greatly resembled. He had the good of his people, and their advancement in knowledge, always at heart, and preferred it, as was subsequently amply proved, even to the ties of blood and the gratification of a domestic affection which could hardly be surpassed. Masiric was a wit and a mimic, and never suffered his high position to hamper his love of drollery; whereas the king possessed a certain dignity which never deserted him, and even under the most trying circumstances preserved him from ridicule.

Even as matters were, and on so short an acquaintance, the captain was disposed to

think well of him, but the news from the
look-out was too serious to be ignored, and
before admitting the visitors to the camp,
he demanded an explanation of it. When
the question was put through the Malay, the
king drew himself up with an offended air,
and the colour rushed into his face. His son
whispered hastily into his ear, and pointed to
Conolly, whereupon his Majesty inclined his
head in haughty assent. Then the midshipman, after a few words with Tarilam,
addressed the captain.

" The king, sir, I am bidden to say,
harbours no thoughts of treachery. He is
at war with his neighbours, and therefore
has been compelled to put to sea with an
escort sufficient to repel any attack that
might be made on him, but coming hither
with all the sentiments of friendship, he
thought it indelicate to alarm your people
by the exhibition of such a formidable fleet.
They are at the back of the island, it is true,
but they are not near enough to save his
Majesty from violence, a contingency which
never so much as entered his mind, and he

regrets that any similar suspicion should, nevertheless, have occurred to you." These words, so uncharacteristic of Master Lewis Conolly, were delivered with a deliberation which, though caused by the difficulty of translation, gave them a certain dignity.

It was now the captain's turn to speechify, a feat in which it must be confessed he was less successful than his royal visitor.

" Well, upon my soul, it was most uncommonly considerate and deuced gentlemanly of the old gentleman," he exclaimed with enthusiasm, "and you may tell him so for me."

This eulogium, rendered, let us hope, less literally than the speech of the prince had been, was received by the monarch with great satisfaction.

" Never," he said, " has the sweet voice of Deltis sounded more grateful to my ears." The captain bowed respectfully, and in an aside with the midshipman, inquired what on earth was meant by *that?* Then Master Conolly, with purple countenance, arising from a pressing tendency to mirth, reminded him that on account of his singing he had been likened to the bird called Deltis, the only one of the feathered tribe in Breda who could favour its inhabitants with a song.

"But you do not sing in the Bredan language, my young shaver, so how is it that these good folks understand you?"

Then the boy modestly explained that Prince Tarilam had taken a fancy to him on his first arrival on the island, and ever since had passed several hours daily in his company, acquiring from him, with the help of the interpreter, the English tongue, for which he had shown a remarkable adaptability, while in so doing he had of necessity imparted something of his own.

"But is this prince of yours and his father to be thoroughly trusted, think you?" inquired the captain, doubtfully; "for my experience as yet has been that the cleverer the savage the greater the rogue."

"There is not a more truthful or kinder-hearted man in England than Prince Tarilam, sir," answered the midshipman warmly, "and he tells me that all the good in him he owes to the teaching of the king."

"Well, well, I hope it may be so; at all events we must chance it," was the captain's conclusion; whereupon he formally invited the visitors to enter the camp.

Then, Master Lewis Conolly calling to mind that there were already two interpreters, and having something on his own account to say to somebody else, slipped away from the *cortége* and ran up to where Edith and Aunt Sophia were standing on a rock a little removed from the rest, but whence they had a good view of the whole proceedings. He was received by both with an excess of welcome, which, if he had been two years older, would certainly not have been accorded to him. He was just at that happy epoch when nobody but yourself knows how old you are, and thoroughly enjoyed the privilege of his position. Aunt Sophia called him indifferently "Mr. Conolly" and "my dear boy," just as the matter on which they were speaking chanced to be familiar or otherwise. Edith, by way of compromise, addressed him as Lewis; but the young rascal was well aware that he was as great a favourite with one as the other.

Aunt Sophia would have had him at once recount his adventures, but this juvenile Ulysses was much too wary to run the risk of wasting their effect at such a juncture. He confined himself to speaking of the exalted individuals who were then sharing their attention with him, and might at any moment monopolize it. He pointed out to them the axes which hung from the shoulders of the king and his son, and which were the ensigns of their royal race. The handles were of ebony, and the blades of shells. Around the wrist of the former was also a bracelet of polished bone, which, though of the simplest material and construction, implied in its wearer the possession of the greatest honour as well as of the highest rank—a combination of the Victoria Cross and the Garter. It was worn also by Prince Masiric, as commander-in-chief.

"But I hope that beautiful Prince Tarilam has got the bone," observed Aunt Sophia.

"He has one, but he is too modest to wear

it," returned the midshipman. "His view is that it is the reward of merit, and that there is no merit, but only a fortunate accident, in being a king's son."

"That is a very noble motive for a savage," remarked Edith, in astonishment.

"A savage! He is no more a savage than —well—I really know no one who would not suffer by comparison with him," cried the boy, with eager enthusiasm. "See, they are about to show them what a musket can do. In spite of all I could say, the Malay would explain the use of the bullet they picked up, and since then they have been wild to hear the 'white man's thunder,' as they call it."

The visitors were now, in great expectancy, assembled round the captain and Mr. Marston, the latter of whom had a musket in his hand. He was the best shot in the ship's company,*

---

* Sailors are seldom good shots. This is the reason why the exploring expeditions sent to the North Seas have suffered so much privation, and is in a great measure the reason of their ill-success. There is a sufficiency of game, if only one could bring it down, which Dr. Rae, with his company of 'trappers'—Hudson's Bay men— never failed to do.

and had therefore been intrusted with the task of impressing upon their new friends the efficacy of firearms. The thunder could be made sure of, of course, but it was essential to demonstrate the effects of the lightning. There was no lack of birds to aim at, albeit they were not of a kind known to European sportsmen; though songless, they were of the most beautiful and gorgeous colours—the men called them flying rainbows—and slid rather than flew through the warm and lustrous air. It seemed "a sin and a shame," as Aunt Sophia said, to kill one, and all the more so since, never having been molested by man, and not understanding his inventions, especially gunpowder, they made no great haste to get out of his reach. It would have made an *habitué* of Wimbledon smile to see the care with which the first mate handled his piece, watched his chance, and then took aim at a bird as bright and big as a peacock, that was leisurely passing over their heads; it was very like a literal rendering of the metaphor, "a barn door flying," and a barn door made more demonstrative by brilliant advertisements; but at all events he hit it, and down it came.

The flash of fire, the noise, and then the fall of the bird, created three distinct sensations in the visitors. Some stopped their ears, some shut their eyes (the better, like Mr. Justice Stareleigh, to exercise their judgment), and even the king suffered himself to be betrayed into an exclamation of astonishment. As for the emotional Masiric—prince and commander-in-chief though he was—he ran after the bird like a retriever, and picking it up, examined it with the most minute attention. How the creature could have been killed without the flame from the gun reaching him, which it clearly had not done, taxed his reason beyond his powers to explain.

Prince Tarilam turned his shapely head towards the rock on which Conolly was standing, and smiled. "You have not the least exaggerated matters," the smiler seemed to say, "but I should like to have one or two things elucidated respecting this amazing incident." The midshipman was at his side in a moment; but while the other lent his ear apparently to scientific information, his gaze was fixed upon the spot which his companion had just left.   Presently Conolly also turned his eyes in the same direction, as a man always does do, sooner or later, if the object of his discourse is visible.

"I do believe the Prince has been asking questions about *us*, and not about the musket at all," ejaculated Aunt Sophia.

"Perhaps he wants to know whether it will kill people as well as birds," said Edith, drily.

"Oh, how wicked! oh, how *can* you!" exclaimed her companion; "I am sure the prince would not hurt a fly.   Moreover, it can't be that, because Mr. Conolly is shaking his head, and very decidedly too."

"That may corroborate my view," persisted Edith; "he is teaching him the rudiments of the sixth commandment."

After a great deal of gesture and interpretation, during which the king maintained an air of extreme gravity and reflection, while Prince Masiric exhibited his powers of imitation of a musket-shot—just as a child presents a

walking-stick and cries, "Pop, bang, fire!"—
the visitors began to prepare for departure.
The captain and the officers held their hands
out, when, much to their astonishment and
a little to their alarm, they were treated to
quite another form of salutation. Each of the
visitors seized his neighbour by the shoulder,
the king holding the captain as in a vice, the
prince seizing the midshipman, and Masiric
clutching Mr. Marston with such hearty good-
will, that he left his mark on him for an hour
afterwards; every host, in fact, was similarly
collared by his guest.

"It is an expression of personal friendship," explained Conolly, hastily, for it was
plain that the demonstration was not being
accepted in the spirit in which it was offered
—"the tighter they grasp you, the higher is
the estimation they have formed of your
character."

"His Majesty must think me an angel,
then," murmured the captain, rubbing his
arms. He smiled, however, with much complacency, as did all the rest, as in duty bound.
It was, moreover, a relief to them to find that

this tenacious treatment, which suggested
perpetual imprisonment, had, after all, a
friendly aim.

Then, amid blowing of conch shells and
splashing of paddles, the king and his suite
departed.   At the mouth of the harbour they
delayed a little, while at a given signal the
fleet, consisting of more than a hundred
canoes, came swiftly up from below the island,
and took their station behind the royal barge,
when the whole *cortége* left for home.   It was
a splendid sight, and a method of royal con-
veyance at least as imposing as the gilt
carriage and eight cream-coloured horses used
on state occasions in our own country.

The two ladies would certainly not have
grudged it their admiration, but for a circumstance which at the moment drew their attention to another quarter.

"See, Mr. Conolly has not gone," cried
Edith, eagerly, who in the confusion and
crowd upon the beach had not hitherto recognized the fact that the midshipman had been
left behind.   "How glad I am they have not
taken him back with them !   Though he *has*

such a belief in their good-will, I much prefer to see him left with us."

"They have left other persons behind them too," exclaimed Aunt Sophia, excitedly; "yes, they certainly have. The prince himself, with two of his people, no doubt as hostages and to show that their intentions are honourable. Now, I call that very nice of them. The idea of having such a Prince Charming for our guest is delightful. And, only look, I protest that that dear boy, who knows how I dote on royalty, is bringing him to talk with us. My dear Edith, I feel all in a flutter."

CHAPTER X.

As the midshipman and the young Prince
of Breda approached the ladies, they could not
help observing the contrast between them,
which, indeed, considering that they were
both favourable types, was as great as contrast
could be. The one was a handsome English
boy, fresh-coloured and blue-eyed, with a
roguish drollery in his face that even the
presence of authority could only mitigate, and
which the nature of the undertaking he had
now on hand intensified to an unusual degree.
The prince, on the other hand, whose come-
liness was of quite another kind, and whose
grace of form suggested some faultless statue,
wore an expression of sedateness altogether
alien to his years. With this, however, was

mingled no touch of austerity ; indeed, it was the tenderness of his looks, joined to a certain worshipful awe as he drew near the young lady, which was trying Master Lewis Conolly's gravity to the utmost.

"The Prince Tarilam wishes to have the honour of your acquaintance, ladies," he observed sedately.

The ladies bowed and held out their hands, which, to their astonishment, he raised respectfully to his lips.   No courtier could have surpassed the grace and ease of it, only he saluted the younger lady first, and perhaps retained her hand a second or two longer.

" Welcome," he said, " to Faybur, and may you be happy with us."   The speech, though so brief, was evidently rehearsed beforehand, and he looked at the midshipman when he had uttered it with the simplicity of a child who seeks approval from his teacher.

" Quite right," exclaimed Conolly, encouragingly.   Then, in lower and more rapid tones, he added, " I was priming his Royal Highness with a lot of pretty speeches as we came along in the canoe, and that is the one he selected.

He is so jolly green that I had not the heart
to keep up the illusion that you were the
goddess of flowers; but he wishes me to
remark that you certainly *are* a flower, Miss
Edith, for all that, and the very fairest he
has ever set eyes on."

Edith blushed and smiled, and deprecatingly
shook her head.

"It is no use denying it like that," observed
the midshipman, gravely, after a brief con-
ference with his companion; "his Royal Highness says he only made a mistake in the kind
of flower; at first he was under the impression
that you were a rose, but he perceives now by
the movement of your head that you are a
lily of the valley."

"You bold, bad boy," cried Aunt Sophia,
"I am quite sure the prince has been saying
nothing of the kind."

At which Edith smiled outright, the midshipman burst into uproarious laughter, and
Tarilam laughed so musically that it seemed
astonishing that so gentle a sound could
proceed from such a formidable frame. There
was no sense of fun in it, of course, yet it was

perfectly natural and genuine, for it arose
from sympathy, just as the countenance of
any kindly-disposed person reflects the spectacle of happiness in others.

"The prince is to be the captain's guest
here for some time, and will share his quarters,"
continued Conolly; "as his host will be occupied with his duties, his Royal Highness
hopes that he may be permitted to call
occasionally in Ladies' Bay, and cultivate your
acquaintance. He would like some of your
leisure time to be spent in teaching him
reading, writing, arithmetic, and the use
of the globes."

"Mr. Conolly," said Edith, severely, "it
is neither good taste nor good manners to
make fun of any guest, especially of one who,
from ignorance of our language, is necessarily
at your mercy."

"Ten thousand pardons, Miss Edith; you
don't know what a beast I seem to myself,
now you have held the looking-glass up to
me," returned the midshipman; "I will
never offend again." His penitence was so
earnest as well as so abject, that Edith could

not but forgive him; she knew that Master
Conolly's crime went no further than in permitting his high spirits to run away with him,
whereas they required a tight hand.

"Now, tell me truly what the prince does
say," she answered.

"Well, I have told him that we have all
duties to do here, except you ladies, and that
I am sure, when we are not at leisure to look
after him, you will be so good as to do so a
little; and especially that you will help him
to learn English, which it is his great desire
to master; indeed, I have not exaggerated
matters, Miss Edith, about his having the
highest regard for you; and I am sure" (this
in a hasty parenthesis) "for your aunt also;
and in spite of all his strange surroundings,
you will find Prince Tarilam to be a thorough
gentleman."

"We are quite sure of that," said Aunt
Sophia, an opinion evoked not less from the
lad's own evident conviction, than from the
demeanour of the prince himself. His position
was an exceptionally trying one, something
like that of the gentleman in the figure

'Pastorelle' in the old quadrille, who had the
utmost difficulty, while dancing alone opposite
two ladies and another man, not to look like
a fool; nay, Tarilam had not even the relief
of movement, but in stillness and silence had
to endure the consciousness of being talked
about by his three companions without understanding one word they said. Yet he never
on the one hand betrayed a trace of awkward-
ness, nor on the other, of a too great audacity,
but remained the personification of unem-
barrassed ease. His expression reminded one
of those admirable specimens of gentleness
among the deaf and dumb, for whom as they
listen in vain, but with a smile of patient
intelligence to the conversation of their more
favoured fellow-creatures, few fail to feel a
touch of tenderness.

For the present, his patience was put to
no further test, for the captain here sent to
say that his guest's quarters were ready for
his inspection, so, with a grace and courtesy
seldom seen out of a minuet, he took his
leave.

"That is the best bred young man that

ever I saw," was Aunt Sophia's remark as
soon as he got out of earshot (though *that*
didn't matter much), "and I do hope we
shall see a great deal of him." As Edith took
no notice of this aspiration, it may at least
be supposed that she had no objection to offer
to it. "I wonder where he gets his clothes
from?" continued Aunt Sophia, naïvely.

At this, both of her companions burst out
laughing. "If we are to teach him English,
you will have an excellent opportunity of
asking him that question, Sophy," observed
Edith.

"But, my dear child, you mistake me; I
don't want to know who is his tailor, but
where the material comes from and what it
is, which, as an attire, becomes him so
admirably."

"I can tell you all about that, ladies," said
the midshipman, demurely, "not, of course,
now, but some day when you may happen
to ask me to dinner, in order to have the
whole story of my adventures in Amrac."

Their curiosity to learn that matter was,
as the young rogue knew, extreme, and he

received his invitation for that very day
accordingly. It was not the first time that
he had partaken of the hospitality of the
tenants of Ladies' Bay, whose house, indeed,
save that of the captain, was the only one of
dimensions sufficient for the entertainment of
guests, and he not only esteemed the honour
very highly, but thoroughly appreciated the
superiority of the food he got there over that
of the midshipmen's mess. The freshest fish
that could be caught, the daintiest bird that
could be snared, was always reserved for the
ladies' table.

It was, therefore, with the sense of having
well dined, and of being made much of, and
of having deserved it, that the young gentleman proceeded that afternoon to narrate his
story to his hostesses, or rather—for he was
somewhat in the position of Canning's knife-
grinder, as to 'story'—to allow what he
had to tell to be elicited from him by the
gentle pressure of inquiry.

"In the very first place," observed Aunt
Sophy, "we are wild to know what the
prince was saying about us before you intro-

duced him, and what was the proposition at which you shook your head so positively ?"

"It is the Amrac custom, Miss Norbury, for every one to choose for himself a personal friend, a ceremony which you saw take place on the beach just now ; and he who is chosen becomes as a brother, to be loved, cherished, and protected by the other to his life's end ; and this honour the Prince Tarilam proposed to himself to confer upon *you*."

" Upon *me ?*" exclaimed Aunt Sophia. " Why, goodness gracious, this is the first time the man has ever set eyes upon me !"

" Once is surely quite enough, madam," returned the midshipman, demurely, " for any man to be impressed with your merits, only as this ceremony involved some physical pain, and was also liable to misconstruction, I persuaded him to perform it by proxy."

"Then who is to take care of my niece ?" inquired Aunt Sophia, with a severity she found it difficult to assume, for the compliment that had been paid her was not displeasing.

"Miss Edith, madam, has been bespoken as a sister by Majuba."

"And who on earth is Majuba?"

"To be sure—that is because you would not let me begin at the beginning. Majuba is the only daughter of King Taril, a most lovely young woman, and as good, I do assure you, as she is beautiful."

"You seem to have a very great insight into character, young gentleman," said Aunt Sophia. "May I ask if you stood proxy for Edith as you did for me, and were pinched by this excellent young person in the shoulder?"

"She did just nip me with her finger and thumb," stammered the young gentleman; "it was like being vaccinated, only it seemed shorter."

"I am afraid it was contagion, however, that you received from it, and not protection," observed Aunt Sophia, with uplifted finger. "Mr. Redmayne was certainly wrong, Edie, when he told us that no midshipman had been ever seen to blush."

"Mr. Redmayne has made up for it since

he became a mate, by blushing whenever a lady speaks to him," returned Master Conolly, contemptuously.

"And how old is this Princess Majuba?" inquired Edith, smiling in spite of herself.

"She is just four years younger than Prince Tarilam, and very like him," replied the midshipman. "She was uncommonly interested in you both, and would have come here to-day, but that it is contrary to etiquette for a woman to accompany the king on a visit of ceremony."

"But tell us all about everything in its proper order," interrupted Aunt Sophia, impatiently; "do let us persuade you—if only temporarily—to drop Majuba."

Master Conolly cast at Aunt Sophia a look of deep reproach—she had always hitherto been his best friend, and this desertion, and especially the rallying of him in the presence of Edith, wounded him to the quick—and then commenced as follows:—

"When the canoe in which I went away approached Amrac, there was a great surf, so that it seemed impossible to land; but somehow the thing was done, and I found myself literally high and dry, for I was carried at once upon men's shoulders, and in the midst of a great concourse of people, to the king's house. I offered him the presents sent by the captain, which he accepted very graciously, and at once began to eat the sweet biscuits and the tea. On the other hand, I was regaled with something like toffee, only very dry and hard, on a tortoise-shell dish ; the Malay told me it was the highest compliment that could be conferred upon me, so I pretended to enjoy it, while the scoundrel himself was eating the most excellent cray-fish and dried turtle, served on plantain leaves.

"I did my best to pretend to like it, but it was hard work, for I was very hungry. Every one else who was eating what pleased him, pretended to look on me with envy, nor did the king himself—though he could hardly be enjoying the dried tea leaves—observe that I was not worthy of so much honour; but directly the prince entered the room, he seemed to understand the whole situation at a glance. He bade me, through the interpreter, put the precious fragments of hard-bake aside as if for future use, and then caused me to be served with more agreeable, if more humble, food.

"It struck one at once, somehow, that here was an intelligent and independent-minded fellow, not in the least affected by forms and ceremonies. Though his manner to his father was full of respect and duty, it seemed to me that the king looked up to him as to a superior mind. At all events, he did what he liked with his Majesty as with everybody else. After the meal was over, he took me into an adjoining room and introduced me to his sister, the princess."

"How was she dressed?" inquired Aunt Sophia.

"In white raiment, like an angel. Her attire was, in fact, of the same material as that you saw worn by the prince, only much fuller and longer; it is made of tappa, a substance beaten out of the bark of a sort of mulberry tree. Every one wears it, and it is always spotless; but washing is extremely cheap in Breda. The interpreters were not admitted to the princess's presence; so, though she and her brother talked together of course, all my intercourse with her was by signs. Yet, you have no idea how well we got on together."

"Indeed we have a very good idea," said Edith, laughing.

"It is all very well to laugh," continued the midshipman, pretending not to understand her, "but though I felt quite safe in the company of these two charming persons, I had no such confidence in the people at large, and I especially mistrusted the Malay."

"We have not yet done with your princess," observed Aunt Sophia, severely; "your interview seems to have been very short. Did nothing else occur than what you have told us?"

"There was a little dance which I forgot to mention," said Master Conolly, with simplicity.

"Oh, indeed, you danced with this young woman, did you?"

"With the princess? Certainly not, madam. But, by way of entertaining me, as I suppose, a number of young ladies, her handmaidens, were summoned, and executed what you might call a ballet."

"But what might *you* call it, sir," inquired Aunt Sophia. "*Was* it a ballet?"

"I rather think it was," confessed the youth, demurely. "They were all dressed in flowers, and very pretty."

"Very pretty," repeated Aunt Sophia, not like an echo, but severely.

"I mean the flowers were very pretty," explained the young gentleman. "But I was very tired and sleepy and hardly looked at anything."

"He means he had no eyes for any one else but the Princess Majuba," observed Edith, smiling.

"I don't know what he means," said Aunt Sophia; "I only know he ought never to have gone to Amrac without somebody to take care of him. Do you mean to say, sir, that you were not asked to sing?"

"Oh, yes, I had forgotten that. The princess—I mean the prince—kept saying 'Deltis, Deltis,' and so I did sing her a song."

"'Rule Britannia,' I dare say," said Aunt Sophia, scornfully; "nothing of a sentimental character, of course."

"Oh, no, I sang her an horticultural song, 'The Last Rose of Summer,' I think it was."

"He has already acquired all the duplicity of the savage," observed Aunt Sophia, lifting up her hands. "Well, *go on*, sir."

CHAPTER XI.

"PRESENTLY I began to yawn, so that the prince burst out laughing, and gave me in charge to one of his male attendants, who showed me where I was to sleep. This was a large room in another house, with a couple of fires in it, for the nights in Amrac are much colder than in Breda. They gave me a mat to lie upon, and another to draw over me, and a block of wood for a pillow. I should have slept soundly enough on it, but for the strangeness of the place, and for the being away from everybody I knew."

"Poor fellow," exclaimed the two ladies, simultaneously; for under the mask of raillery and pretended severity, Aunt Sophia felt at least as tenderly for the boy as Edith.

"Then, in the middle of the night, eight men came in and made up the fires, preparatory, as I thought, to roasting me at one of them, but it was only, as it turned out, an excess of civility and attention, and soon after daybreak they brought me yams and cocoanuts and some turtle soup for breakfast, which I partook of in the presence of about five hundred men and women, all sitting round me in perfect silence, and waiting, as the interpreter presently told me, for a song.

"The people at large seemed to care for nothing but singing and flowers, and though very kind and pleasant, could not understand that one could not sing for ever, even on turtle soup. I was so tired and weary, that when the king came down and wanted more singing, I had hardly strength to comply with his request, but made signs that I wanted to return to Faybur to recover my voice. Whereupon he pointed up to the trees, and blew strongly with his mouth; and, to indicate what would happen in such weather if the canoes should venture out, he joined his hands together, with the palms upwards, and turning them the reverse way, signified that they would overset. Then he said, 'Deltis,' indicating how I should employ the time, for a month or two, till the fair weather set in, and I, on my part, resolutely shut my mouth and shook my head.

"Then the prince came full of intelligence and consideration, and smiles that seemed to take disappointment away from everybody, and took me by the hand to his own house.

"There I found the two interpreters, our own and the Malay, from the latter of whom the prince had already learnt a few words of English, and we set to work to make ourselves intelligible to one another. Never did I see so quick a scholar. In less than a week he knew at least three times as much of my language as I did of his, and long before I came away we dispensed with the interpreter altogether. The king, on the other hand, was rather a dunce at it, he said he was too old a dog to learn new tricks."

"My dear Mr. Conolly, he surely never said *that,*" expostulated Edith.

"No, no, it was what he would have said, I

mean, if he could have said anything; but the prince and I got on famously."

"And Majuba?" demanded Aunt Sophia, inexorably; "was she not also a pupil?"

"To be sure, I had forgotten that; when I said that the prince was the quickest scholar I had ever seen, I should have said the quickest male scholar; the princess beat him into fits."

"What imagery!" murmured Aunt Sophia. "How true it is that poetry is the natural language of love! And when you had taught this peerless young person to talk, may I ask what it was you talked about?"

"I think you are rather hard upon our young friend, Sophy," remonstrated Edith. "Remember, Mr. Conolly, that you are not obliged to criminate yourself, if you find any difficulty in replying to that question."

"I find none at all," retorted the young gentleman, audaciously; "I talked to the princess about *you*. She was immensely interested, and I told her everything."

"About *me?*" exclaimed Edith; her tone was not only one of surprise, but of annoyance.

"All about both of you," he answered hurriedly, "how you had embarked on board ship for India, and were shipwrecked, and were now in Breda all alone."

"Oh, I see," cried Edith, with an air of ill-concealed relief; "and she was kind and sympathizing, was she?"

"She was, indeed; she would have come to you at once, as I have said, if etiquette had permitted it."

"You do not seem to have been much inconvenienced by etiquette yourself," observed Aunt Sophia, drily.

"Was I not? Wait till the king delights to honour *you*, madam (as I am sure he will), and gives you hard-bake," replied the youth innocently. "As for the princess, she will be here—weather permitting—to-morrow or the next day."

"Faybur has, doubtless, new attractions for her, which it had not before," remarked Aunt Sophia, viciously.

"Yes, madam," was the demure rejoinder, "she cannot bear being separated from her only brother."

"You have said that you mistrusted the Malay," observed Edith, after a pause. "Why was that?"

"Well, I can hardly say; it is, perhaps, only a case of 'I do not like thee, Dr. Fell,' but still I found out one thing from our own interpreter during my first day at Breda, that it was not on that island, as he told us, on which the Malay had been shipwrecked, but on Amrac, and that the people there did not kill him, but suffered him to escape to Breda, which is suspicious, as showing a fellow-feeling with the refugee."

"The Amrac folks are very wicked, I suppose, then?"

"A pack of murderers, nothing less."

"What a partisan our young friend has become," observed Aunt Sophia. "I dare say if the truth were known, there are princes and princesses in Amrac quite as respectable —to say the least of it—as in Breda."

Master Conolly shook his head, and in tones much more serious than he had hitherto used, assured his companions that this was not the case. "From Amrac," he said, "there is everything to fear, a nation delighting in bloodshed, and because no treaty can bind them, always at war with their neighbours."

"And they might come over here some fine day," observed Aunt Sophia, apprehensively.

"Well, any fine day—for they are not such good sailors as the Breda folks. Yes. There is no fear, however, but that we shall be able to give a good account of them," said the midshipman, drawing himself up to his full five feet.

Here a messenger came from the captain to summon Mr. Conolly, to relieve him from his duties for an hour or two in the entertainment of the prince; whereupon he vanished at once.

"Poor Captain Head finds conversation with his Royal Highness a little difficult, no doubt," observed Aunt Sophia.

"I should hardly think that, after Mr. Conolly's account of his proficiency in English; he must have understood us, I fancy, a great deal better than we thought he did."

"Gracious goodness! Do you really think so, Edith? What a horrible notion! What was that we said about his clothes?"

"You mean what was that *you* said?" returned Edith, laughing.

"Dear, dear! it makes one quite hot to
think of it! What a mischievous monkey
that boy is."

The afternoon, though fine as usual, was
somewhat oppressive, and when it was so it
was the custom of the ladies to bathe in a
sheltered cove at the extremity of the little
bay. It was a reflection they had often made,
that though their whole wardrobe had been
safely landed, the articles which they had
heretofore been accustomed to set most store
by, such as their dinner and ball dresses, were
now utterly useless, while their more homely
garments were become of great value; of
these none were more useful than their bathing
gear, which enabled them to take a bath of
the most enjoyable kind whenever they felt
inclined for it. Edith was a tolerable proficient in natation, and, under the new condi-
tions of the sea and air and sand, enjoyed it
as she had never done before, while her aunt
watched her with envy from the shallows.
Beside the five senses, there are various

channels for the influx of human happiness, not so common to all, but which, nevertheless, many foolishly despise or ignore, who have it in their power to use them. One of these is the art of swimming, the neglect of which in an age of so-called ' culture' and education, and one which prides itself on squeezing all that is pleasant out of life to the last drop, both for man and woman, is inexplicably neglected by the latter. At the date of our story, this was of course still more the case. It had been her father's custom, however— itself a rare one at the time—to spend at least a month every year by the sea-side, and there Edith had acquired this accomplishment. Enjoyable as she had found it at Ramsgate and Dover, it was ten times more so at Breda; where the buoyancy of the sea, the purity of the air, the brilliancy of the sky, and the exquisite beauty of the surrounding scenery, joined to that forgetfulness of trouble produced by the exercise itself, made her in truth more happy when in the water than she ever felt out of it.

Aunt Sophia splashed about well within her

depth, with a much inferior sense of pleasure, and with a certain groundless apprehension on her niece's account, such as a hen might feel who has hatched a duckling. She was constantly entreating her niece not to swim so far out, as though increased depth meant increased danger, and I am afraid that Edith took some malicious pleasure—as experts will do under such circumstances—in arousing her fears. On the present occasion, she was disporting herself as usual, some distance from the shore, when a cry from Aunt Sophia reached her. She laughingly replied that she was all right, and, to prove it, took another stroke or two out to sea. Then the cry was repeated, and this time it struck her that there was something unusual in it. It was not the warning note of apprehension, but the shrill treble of agonized alarm. She looked back and beheld her companion standing on the shore, and pointing with a vehemence that also somehow signified despair, to some object between herself and the swimmer.

Edith's eyes followed the direction of her gaze, saw something twinkle in the water, and

then disappear. She knew it at once for what
it was, for on board ship she had seen it many
times, and never—though herself in perfect
safety—without a shudder of fear ; it was the
brown fin of a shark.

Fear seized her soul, and for a moment
so paralyzed her limbs that she was in imminent danger of sinking : if she could have
sunk, and been drowned before the creature
came up with her, she felt that it would
have been well indeed. It was not so long
ago that she had felt that death in any form
would have been welcome to her ; but that
hopeless mood had of late been passing away,
and at no time, indeed, could she have confronted such a form of death as *this* without
horror and aversion. The most miserable
among us who yearns to be " anywhere, anywhere out of the world," would shrink from
such a gate of exit. Not even unconscious-
ness, which generally mitigates a shock of
horror so intense and sudden, stepped in to
her relief. The vitality, that for an instant
had deserted her frame, returned to it, and
with it an only too accurate understanding of

her helpless position. The shark was between her and the shore. No boat could possibly reach her as soon as it, and indeed no man, if man could be found to run for her sake upon certain death. The sentry on the rampart had, indeed, as usual been withdrawn upon the ladies expressing their intention of bathing, and no one apparently was in earshot of her aunt's passionate cries for help.

All this she took in at a glance, as it were mechanically, but her whole power of thought was concentrated on her unseen enemy. We are told that when sudden death lays hold upon us—as when, for example, those lose consciousness who are about to drown—that a vision of our past sweeps through the mind, and we seem to live our life again at the very moment of quitting it; but this was not the case with Edith Norbury. Her eyes as she swam desperately shoreward, were fixed with agonized intentness on the sea, and her soul was monopolized by the thought of the hateful creature that was lying in wait therein to rend her. When she should see that brown fin rise again, it would be the sign, she knew, that death in its most appalling form was close upon her.

At present it was probable that the shark was not aware of her proximity; he had, indeed, been swimming close in shore, and had snapped at that not unconscious trifle Aunt Sophia, just as she ran out of his reach; but it was to the last degree unlikely that having found bathers about, he would not be looking for more. Still there was hope—without which she could not have swum a stroke—that he might have gone elsewhere.

Edith positively was not fifty yards from the sandy beach, and was straining every nerve to reach it, when something close beside her rose out of the water, and sideways with a gleaming flash, made at her; then she uttered one despairing shriek and knew no more.

CHAPTER XII.

PRINCE TARILAM had been right royally received by Captain Head; entertained with the choicest pickled meats and other European delicacies, including champagne—which he had declined to swallow in an effervescing state upon the ground that living things were neither drunk nor eaten in Breda—and welcomed as hospitably as guest could be; but conversation had flagged between his host and him. He could not use his newly-acquired tongue with others with the same freedom as with Conolly, who understood his peculiar difficulties with it, and could help him out of them. He was diffident, too, as some of us, though not naturally shy, are apt to be when talking to a Frenchman who is not our tutor; and everything was so new and strange that the attention which it was so necessary to pay to his companion's speech was constantly being diverted elsewhere. So when he had delivered certain messages from the king, full of amity and concord, and these had been reciprocated, both parties felt their conversational powers on the wane.

"I can't be talking to this blessed prince all day about the greatness and goodness of his father," was the captain's impatient reflection, "so I'll get young Conolly to take him off my hands."

At the mention of the midshipman, the prince brightened up at once, as the face of the after-dinner guest is gladdened by the offer of an unexpected cigar, and the proposal that his young friend should take him round the camp was accepted with pleasure. Except that the summons withdrew him from the society of the ladies, the midshipman was equally pleased to be his cicerone.

There are few things more pleasant than to introduce a person, for whom one has a liking, to objects of interest, which, though familiar to ourselves, are unknown to them; it is something like the sensation of telling an excellent but well-known joke to a new audience. Everything in the prince's eyes was novel and amazing, down to the very grindstone on which the men's swords were sharpened. The glitter of their bayonets—for he had never seen any polished body, or the action of light upon it—delighted him. A small hatchet which Conolly gave him, and which he compared with his own axe of shell with quite a piteous sense of its inferiority, filled him with gratitude. His observation was ceaseless, and so keen, and even deep, that a superficial explanation did not serve his turn, and it was not always easy to satisfy his curiosity. Like Columbus, he had discovered a new world, but, unlike him, one much more marvellous and in a far higher stage of civilization than the one with which he was familiar.

Their walk extended beyond the camp, to the outworks of Ladies' Bay. "Why is there no sentinel here, as elsewhere," inquired the prince, whose quick eye noticed what was absent as well as what was present. Conolly explained to him, that in order to afford greater privacy, the sentry was withdrawn when the ladies were bathing.

"Bathing!" he cried in his own dialect. "Are they bathing there?" From his tone, which was one of alarm, Conolly gathered there was something seriously amiss, but knew not what. "Tetmil, tetmil," exclaimed Tarilam excitedly. Conolly knew that this was the term in Breda for a shark, and his heart sank within him. Before he could reply, an agonized shriek broke from the shore, where, a quarter of a mile away, he suddenly caught sight of a figure in blue serge, wildly gesticulating. The next instant he was alone.

Literally like an arrow from a bow, Tarilam had left his side, and was flying along the sands with a speed that almost outstripped the power of vision. Master Lewis Conolly was a good runner, and to leap from the rampart and follow his late companion was the work of a moment, but he might as well have matched himself against the wind. Aunt Sophia, almost out of her mind with terror, was conscious only of something white flashing by her like a gigantic gull, and plunging into the sea. In truth, there was need of speed beyond what lies in the thews and sinews of ordinary men. Edith's shriek, and, perhaps, some mechanical beating of her arm through excessive terror, had momentarily frightened the shark—the most cowardly of all predatory creatures—and caused it to miss its aim; when it turned to come at her again, with gleaming teeth and ravening maw, it found a less helpless foe.

Almost as much at home in water as on land, and not unused to such combats, Tarilam awaited its rush, and at the moment of impact swerved aside, and buried his hatchet in the creature's head with a force that needed no second blow. Then, bearing up Edith's inanimate form with his left arm, and oaring himself with the other to the shore, he laid her at Aunt Sophia's feet, with the dumb delight of a retriever.

The whole affair had happened within so short a space that Conolly only just reached the spot in time to aid in restoring the girl to consciousness, a task to which Miss Norbury alone would have been quite unequal. Her nerves had by no means recovered the frightful shock to which they had been subjected, and, indeed, the spectacle of her niece's preserver, whose white garment was covered with blood from his dead foe, was not of a nature to restore them. Either fearing the effects of his appearance upon her, or by a delicate intuition recognizing that his further services could just then be dispensed with, the prince quietly re-entered the water, and busied himself in removing the stains of combat from his apparel.

Edith came to herself with a shudder, and looked about her like one who is doubtful of her own identity; the truth was she could not understand, with the recollection of the horrible fate that had seemed so certain and so imminent, how it had come to pass that she was still in life and unharmed.

"That dear prince has saved you," sobbed Aunt Sophia, replying to her wondering look. "He has the swiftness of a deer and the courage of a lion; no other human being could have done it."

"That is quite true," observed the young midshipman sorrowfully. "I was of no use at all."

Edith held out her hand and smiled feebly. "I am sure you did what you could," she murmured.

"Oh, yes, I ran like a snail," he answered sorrowfully; "now, perhaps, you will believe what I told you ladies of Prince Tarilam. There are very few princes at home, I fancy, who would run like that to meet a shark in his native element."

It might have been rejoined with some reason that such feats were out of the line of European princes, but neither lady was in the humour to throw cold water on the boy's enthusiasm, nor to detract, however indirectly, from the merits of his hero.

"Tell me how it all happened," cried Edith, her eyes wandering gratefully to her unconscious preserver.

Master Conolly obeyed, describing with no little dramatic force, because with perfect naturalness, what had taken place; then perceiving that Edith was greatly moved, and apparently distressed by the narrative, he added with an attempt at jocularity, "I do hope that in future you ladies will be more careful where you bathe."

"Bathe!" cried Aunt Sophia, vehemently, "I doubt whether I shall ever dare again even to wash. The creature came up to within a foot of me, my dear Edie, before it went off to you." Edith shuddered again, then murmured with emotion,

"How can I ever tell him what I owe him?"

"It is unnecessary," observed the midship-man confidently. "One look of thanks, if I know him, will tell him all you feel. He thinks much less of what he has done, believe me, than we think of it. What is distressing him just now, on the other hand, is a matter that you will only smile at. Though the people of Breda are almost amphibious, they dislike above all things getting wet. A shower of rain, which fortunately seldom occurs, will keep the whole nation within-doors, and the prince, I will wager, was much less concerned about the shark than about getting his clothes wet in killing him."

As Conolly completed his explanation, Tarilam, his attire dried in the soft air and sunshine, and freed from the stains of combat, came up with a quiet smile of congratulation.

"I hope miss is not much worse," he said; a sentence which it is probable was not altogether extempore; indeed, he had been repeating it to himself for some time by the sea-shore, like Demosthenes, before he ventured upon its deliverance in public.

"I should have been *dead* but for your timely aid," said Edith, holding out her hand, which Tarilam took with great respect, and bowed over like a bronze Chesterfield. "I shall never forget that I owe you my life, prince."

"I did nothing," said Tarilam, with a disclaiming wave of the hand. "Thanks to my friend here"—he touched the boy lightly on the shoulder—"who gave me this hatchet, it was very small work; if Deltis" (a word he pronounced with extraordinary sweetness) "could have run as fast, he would have done as well."

He spoke slowly and with difficulty, but in the gentlest tone; it was evident, by the expression of his face, that he wished the young fellow to share whatever honour was to be derived from the late proceedings.

"That is a very big 'if,'" observed the midshipman. "I don't know what I should have done, even had I come up in time and been in your place. I am afraid the shark would have eaten both me and the young lady."

Edith shuddered. The prince perceived it, and at once assumed a tone of indifference. "In Breda we think nothing of tetmils," he said, "there are one, two, three—a thousand of them everywhere."

"That only makes it worse," observed Aunt Sophia.

"What he means," explained Conolly slyly, "is that your first shark always makes an impression, sometimes a very serious one."

"I cannot laugh with you, Mr. Conolly," said Edith; "I have been too near and too lately at death's door."

"And such a door!" remarked Aunt Sophia naïvely.

The prince looked interrogatively from one to the other.

It is only the alien who notes how much even the most ordinary conversation teems with metaphor.

The helplessness of this magnificent creature in the toils of small talk moved the pity of both the ladies, and helped him to find a way to their hearts almost as much as his heroism. What also struck them very favourably was that the curiosity which consumed his fellow-countrymen seemed to be absent in his case, at all events, as regarded themselves. He took everything belonging to them as a matter of course, even their bathing dresses. In this last matter it is probable that they did him more than justice, since, to Prince Tarilam's eyes, whatever they wore must have appeared an excess of apparel; but the fact was, that while observant enough of externals, he attached little of that importance to them which, while among ourselves it is the indication of a weak nature, is everywhere the characteristic of an uncivilized race.

"Don't you think, Edith," whispered Aunt Sophia, after a pause that would have been embarrassing to almost any stranger, but

which the visitor endured with all the *sang
froid,* and twice the grace of a royal equerry,
"don't you think we ought to ask him to
tea?"

The notion of meeting the occasion in such
a very conventional way drew a smile to the
girl's face, which was immediately reflected in
that of Tarilam.

"I shall have much pleasure to come," he
said, with gentle earnestness.

"Now, how could he possibly have heard
me?" exclaimed Aunt Sophia, wonderingly.
"Did *you* hear me, Mr. Conolly?"

"No!" replied the midshipman laughing,
"but Prince Tarilam can hear the grass grow
and the buds blossom; if you wish to say anything you don't want him to hear, I warn you
that you had better write it down. Then you
will be safe."

The prince smiled sadly, threw out his
hands with childish pathos, and shook his
head. If he had said, "There, indeed, you
have the advantage of poor me," he could not
have expressed himself more clearly.

"We must really teach him to write,

my dear," observed Aunt Sophia, *sotto voce.*

"If you will please to be so good," said Tarilam humbly.

"Drat the man," murmured Aunt Sophia, this time taking good care to be inaudible, "one cannot open one's lips within a mile of him, without his catching one up."

The acuteness of the prince's senses was indeed amazing, and it had been brought to perfection by practice; that of his intelligence was also not less abnormal, but hitherto it had necessarily been dormant; and though "Knowledge to his eyes her ample page, rich with the spoils of time, had ne'er unrolled," he longed to read it. This species of ambition is very rare among those we call savages, and, indeed, with uneducated people of all sorts, who generally seek to excuse their ignorance by a pretence of indifference. Tarilam had none of this pinchbeck stoicism; it was not often that in the contemplation of a novelty, however amazing, he lost his dignity, but there were occasions when he did so. This happened, for example, on his first introduction to the ladies' little parlour, where the mirror which had once ornamented the cuddy of the *Ganges* was let into the wall.

It was curious, as the spectators of the circumstances afterwards agreed, that the mere sight of a perpendicular reflector—for with a horizontal one he must, of course, have been familiar—should have so moved him ; perhaps it struck him as hanging water, but his delight at it was like that of a child.

Aunt Sophia and Conolly were greatly amused, but Edith was not so ; it seemed somehow in one of whom she had begun to form a high ideal like a degradation ; she was glad of the excuse of their having to change their attire, to withdraw from a scene that was nothing less than distressing to her. When she returned the prince had exhausted his admiration of the mirror, and was entranced by another object ; he was standing with a little unframed water-colour drawing in his hand, and discoursing of it to the midshipman ; she caught the words, " Tetmil, Tetmil," repeated with great eagerness, as she entered the room.

"The prince is charmed with your picture of the bathing cove, Miss Edith," explained Conolly.

"It is a compliment to me that he should have recognized it," she replied modestly. His approval would somehow have been more welcome to her—though she owned to herself that this feeling was unreasonable—had it been less extravagant; but as Tarilam had never seen a picture, which seemed to him a species of magic, it was no wonder that the counterfeit presentment of a place he knew, on canvas, aroused his amazement.

Upon being informed that neither Aunt Sophia nor the midshipman could paint, he evinced unmistakable satisfaction. To have found that the whole race to which this enchantress belonged was dowered with the same gift would have given him, perhaps, an impression of his own inferiority too hopeless and discouraging, just as the reflection that "there are forty poets in Paisley" must strike despondency to the hearts of its neighbour towns. The difficulty which the guest experienced in communicating his ideas did not, on the other hand, rouse in Edith any sense of shortcoming, while the obvious distress which his failure to do so sometimes caused him awoke her sympathy.

The reason why so many people find pleasure in foreign travel, though only slightly acquainted with foreign tongues, is that neither at home nor abroad have they any particular thoughts to communicate; they are well content to be understood by the waiters; whereas the struggle with Tarilam at this early period was to render adequately and intelligibly, not only the inferences and conclusions he drew from the novel objects around him, but his own views and opinions.

CHAPTER XIII

MR. BATES FINDS HIS MASTER.

It was amazing how soon, with the more cultured of his new friends at Faybur, and especially with the ladies, Prince Tarilam made himself at home. His very unlikeness, because it consisted mainly in an excessive simplicity, facilitated assimilation, and made it as easy to get on with him as with a truthful child. In matters that were within their common cognizance, on the other hand, he exhibited an extraordinary natural sagacity, while every accession of knowledge added to his attractions as a companion.

With the sailors, however, this was not altogether the case. They had the usual prejudice of their class which induces them to apply the term 'nigger'—however obviously inapplicable—to all persons not born of

European parents, and causes them to be more sceptical even than the hereditary aristocrat of the nobility of nature. Some of them were jealous of the favour which the new-comer enjoyed with their superiors, and some resented the stranger's marvellous physical gifts, which threw those of their best runners and swimmers and climbers completely into the shade. As time went on, however, and Tarilam's generous nature began to be recognized, these antagonistic sentiments remained only among those comparatively few with whom superiority of any kind, but especially that of moral worth, is always offensive. Even the two attendants that remained with him were treated for his sake with a civility which the captain's express commands would have otherwise failed to secure to them. It would have been hard, indeed, had it not been so, for they gave no trouble, and when not employed in ministering to the needs of their young master made themselves generally useful in a hundred ways.

A small canoe had been left with them, and they taught the men such arts of propelling it without stretcher or rowlock as seemed impossible till they themselves had learnt the accomplishment; they showed them how to catch fish by novel methods, and how, when caught, to smoke them, so as to make provision for the future; how to make rope as strong as cables out of the parasitic creepers, that hung like cobwebs from the trees; how to make mats and baskets; and to express from certain fruits a sherbet which they would have pronounced excellent had it but had a little rum in it. Nay, at the captain's request, these good-natured fellows even gave rudimentary lessons in the planting of yams, though they thought it, in common with all other useful labour, very literally *infra dig.* and only suitable for women.

All this time, while the harbour at Faybur remained like a mill-pond above the mill, and the little island basked in sunshine and soft airs, the open sea was so high and rough that all communication was cut off with Breda. The prince and his two attendants were as completely separated from their own belongings as though they had been exiles, and, so

far as he was concerned, he became every day
more naturalized, and familiar with his new
surroundings.   In old times he had had
thoughts, which the traditions and supersti-
tions of his people had forbidden him to en-
courage, of annexing Faybur to the paternal
dominions; and though it was now no longer
in his power to do so, he found an attraction
in it, such as his native isle did not possess.
He passed most of his time at what might be
called the seminary in 'Ladies' Bay,' where he
showed an extraordinary facility in acquiring,
like a child at a dame's school, not only the
rudiments of the English tongue, but 'the
three R's.'   Hitherto his method of computa-
tion had been of the simplest; as many as
one's eyes; as many as a crow's toes; as
many as one's fingers.   Both hands and one
over made eleven, and was the limit of calcu-
lation.   The feathers of a bird, the waves of
the sea, and the number of stars in the firma-
ment had all been for him just eleven.

He could now tot up to millions, and if the
achievement gave him no great advantage,
he derived an immense satisfaction from the

curriculum that carried him thither. Never
had pupil more kindly teachers than had he
in the two ladies; never had tutors a more
eager or grateful pupil. His difficulties,
though they were often absurd, were never
laughed at, with one exception. He had a
difficulty, as many of us have at home, though
of a different kind, with the letter *h*, which
even his musical voice could never pronounce
soft enough; and it was a never-ending joke
with his gentle preceptors that he always
addressed one of them as Aunt Soapy.

When he accompanied them in their rambles,
like a Sandford and Merton rolled into one,
attended by two female Mr. Barlows, his
education was still continued, so that he learnt
as much out of school as in it; and, what was
rather significant, had it been worth any one's
while to observe it, when he was not walking
with the ladies he preferred to walk by himself. It would be interesting to know, could
one have got to "the back of mind," what the
thoughts of this singular being were occupied
with on these occasions. It is certain that
(in one sense, at least) he did not think much

of his ancestors. Though the descendant of a
long line of kings, their power seemed but
paltry, their aims ignoble, and their exploits
of little worth. Culture, indeed, had had an
effect on him very different from the result
which it too often produces among ourselves ;
he was not puffed up by his newly-acquired
superiority over his own race, but rather de-
pressed by the sense of what was lacking in
them and by his own inferiority to those about
him ; he had escaped being a prig (if one can
imagine a Breda prig), because he was not
cultured beyond his wits. What he had acquired, vast as it was in comparison with his
previous knowledge, had but convinced him
how much he had yet to learn. Yet there is
reason to believe that his reflections were not
all despondent. It is no evidence of vanity
to be conscious of our own dormant powers.
Æsop felt it in slavery, and Keats at the
horse jobber's ; not that Tarilam was either
philosopher or poet, but only that he felt
himself fit for something beyond bestowing
toffee on Royal favourites, or even distribut-
ing Orders of the Bone to meritorious man-

slayers. If his vague and simple aspirations could have been put into words, they might have found appropriate expression in the poetic phrase, "Better fifty years of Europe than a cycle of Cathay;" albeit that yet unwritten line was not more unknown to him than Europe was. He was conscious only that beyond the sea somewhere there was another world, peopled with beings of a higher nature than his own, and whose life was more worth living. It may be he was wrong; "the wild joys of life," the dive through the "league-long rollers," and the coming up through the blue wave beyond it, the rush, dart in hand, through the air, on the ranks of the foe, the fray, and the feast, may be worth all our lacquer and gilding, but, if so, Tarilam erred in good company and from no ignoble instinct.

Thus thoughtfully was he strolling one morning along the cliff top that looked towards Breda, and at a distance from the camp, which, considering the nature of the ground, would have taken an ordinary walker some time to cover, when he suddenly perceived Mr. Bates coming towards him. The figure of the third mate was, of course, familiar to him, but there was something in the movements of the man that puzzled him. He was gesticulating violently; holding up his hand as if to forbid his further advance, and shouting with discordant emphasis.

"Stop," he cried, "you something nigger." Then came an oath such as Tarilam had sometimes heard from the sailors, but the meaning of which he could never understand, for swearing is a product of civilization, and was unknown in Breda. "Keep where you are, I say; we don't want any prying savages hereabouts."

Tarilam could perceive the man was angry, but had no conception of the cause, nor did it give him any disquietude. What monopolized his attention was the strangeness of his gait—he lurched and swayed as he came on, and occasionally stumbled. If Tarilam had ever seen a horse with the staggers—but he had never even seen a horse, or evolved the idea of one out of the depths of his own consciousness—it would have reminded him of Mr. Bates, but if he had ever seen a man attempting to walk when very drunk, a still more perfect parallel would have occurred to him.

"Hi, hi! you; stop, I say." By this time the two had met; and Mr. Bates, with a flushed face and protruding eyes, had placed himself straight—or as straight as he could—before him, so as effectually to bar his progress. "Now just you go home again."

"Go home," repeated the prince, with mild surprise. "Why should I go home?"

"Well, there are a thousand reasons, but one will do. Because we don't want any blown-up-with-gunpowder niggers here. Now just be off." Of the exact sense of the man's words, stammered and hiccoughed as they were, there might have been easily some doubt, but about the tone in which they were uttered there could be none at all. If Tarilam had been a dog which had been bidden to go home by a brutal and ill-tempered master, he could not have been addressed more insultingly. Into the bronzed cheek of the prince there suddenly came a vivid colour, and into his soft eyes a flash of flame, which had Mr. Bates been in his usual frame of mind—which was inclined to prudence—would have warned him of danger like a signal fire. But the third mate was in an abnormally heroic state, full of ire, and also of the courage called Dutch.

" Look here," he stuttered, " you nigger, you'll have to go, and if you make me speak again you'll not do it with a whole skin. It is bad enough that you and those other two dusky devils should be kept in camp, holding your heads up and thinking yourselves the equals of Christian men, not to mention of officers and gentlemen like myself, but that you should come peeping and prying out of bounds here is intolerable. Go home, I say."

" No." The monosyllable was uttered gently, but with a determination which was unmistakable; and the speaker looked straight into the other's eyes as he said it. The quietness of expression in his face added, no doubt, to the temptation of its proximity, and Mr. Bates struck him on the mouth with the back of his hand. The next moment he was swaying in air, with a consciousness of space about

him, and of a fall of about four hundred feet
sheer upon a rocky beach.

Mr. Bates's hair, in the absence of any
barber, had grown long, and the other had
seized him by it, as one takes a rabbit by
the ears, and swung him off the cliff top.
Face to face with the terrors of instant death,
the drunken wretch was sobered in a moment;
his tongue clave to the roof of his mouth, and
his limbs grew limp like those of a dead man
on the gallows-tree, but all his senses were
keen enough.

He heard a sudden voice a long way off
cry, "Tarilam! Tarilam!" in a tone of earnest
entreaty, and he knew that the midshipman
Conolly was pleading for his life. Never did
eavesdropper listen to a conversation not
intended for his private ear with a greater
attention than this gentleman *sus per col* paid
to the subsequent dialogue.

"Let him go, let him go," hallooed the
midshipman. Mr. Bates, when he heard
that phrase, reflected with a pang upon the
indefiniteness of the English tongue; the
prince might very well have taken the words

as an encouragement to drop him, instead of pulling him up. "Don't kill him! spare him!" shouted the midshipman, whose voice as it grew nearer unhappily became less distinct through want of breath.

"He struck me," answered the prince irresolutely, and without turning his head. He seemed to be selecting the most jagged rock for the reception of the body of Mr. Bates, which was oscillating under his hand like a pendulum. "No man has ever struck Tarilam and lived to say so."

"For *my* sake, for *my* sake," urged the midshipman, "I beseech you not to let him fall."

"You are my chosen friend; I can refuse you nothing," murmured the prince, regretfully; and with no more effort than it costs a sailor to heave the lead, he landed the third mate upon terra firma, where he lay, though he was not so inanimate as he looked, like a sack just dropped from a crane.

"How did it happen? What did he quarrel with you about?" inquired Conolly, hurrying up, and gazing with amazement on the prostrate mate.

"I don't know," answered Tarilam, gloomily. "He wandered in his walk, and stumbled in his talk, and was angry, and then he gave me a blow. I shall feel it here," and he touched his mouth, "as long as I live."

"It has not marked you," replied Conolly, naïvely—in the midshipman's mess blows were not uncommon in those days, nor the demands of honour very exacting—"but you may depend upon it, he will never boast of it—will you, sir?" This appeal he made to Mr. Bates himself in answer to a glance of adhesion from that gentleman to the promise thus made on his behalf.

"I will never, never boast of it," he murmured earnestly. "The prince may take his davey of that?"

Indeed, it was pretty clear that, as regards recent proceedings, Mr. Bates had not very much to boast *of;* and might well be trusted to be silent for his own sake.

"Come, let us go back to camp," said Conolly persuasively.

With a quiet gesture of assent, Tarilam turned away, and without so much as a glance at his still prostrate foe, began to retrace his steps. Mr. Bates's eyes, like those of a snake in the grass, followed him with an expression of concentrated malignity, which also included his young preserver.

"To-day for you, my friends," he muttered, between his teeth, "to-morrow for me."

It would have been better for all parties, himself included, had Mr. Bates been permitted to obey the laws of gravity.

It may be taken, as a rule, that the time which is given to an unmitigated scoundrel to repent himself in is passed in some occupation of quite another kind, and Mr. Bates was no exception to it. A bad man's life is like a bad novel; the third volume is generally the worst part of it; and there is little cause for regret if its conclusion is what the reviewers describe as 'hurried.'

CHAPTER XIV.

LET US KILL THE NIGGER.

LIFE in Faybur, though for the most part uneventful enough, did not run quite so smoothly with Captain Head and his officers as, thanks to their solicitude, it was made to do for the two ladies. That that private still, the existence of which Edith had so unconsciously betrayed to Mr. Marston, was from time to time at work somewhere, though its whereabouts—for the scene of its operations was easily shifted—had hitherto remained undiscovered, was certain; half a dozen cases of drunkenness had come under the notice of the authorities, and given them great disquietude. Their anxiety would have been even greater had it not seemed pretty clear that the offence was confined to a few of the sailors only; not, as was rightly concluded, that every man Jack of them after so prolonged an abstinence would not have got drunk if he could, but that those who had so ingeniously invented the means of indulging themselves in that luxury took care to keep the secret to themselves. The wisdom of this reticence was unquestionable, for, as matters stood, it was difficult to punish even those who were manifestly guilty of the offence in question.

"It is all very well," Messrs. Murdoch, Rudge, and Mellor would stutter, when accused of being intoxicated—and it was these three men who most frequently fell under that suspicion—"but how is it possible for a fellow to get drunk when every drop of liquor is under lock and key in the doctor's tent?" They continued to attribute their condition to the effect of the climate upon their respective systems, and except that there was a kettle missing, the uses of which it was not judicious for 'the court' to point out to the public at large, there was really no means of refuting this line of defence. The gravity of the danger, however, was fully recognized; and while each instance of delinquency was hushed up as much as possible, not a stone was left unturned to discover the root of the mischief.

Of all this the two ladies were blissfully ignorant, and though Edith, as we know, had her own views of the doubtful tenure on which authority existed in Faybur, the matter had of late months troubled her but little. One could not say that her thoughts were fixed elsewhere, but they had wandered with more or less persistency in another direction. The arrival of Prince Tarilam had very agreeably broken the monotony of life in Ladies' Bay. It had from the first been a pleasure to teach him, so far as she was competent to do so, those "Fairy Tales of Science" and "Long Results of Time," the simplest details of which had for him the attributes of a miracle and the attractions of magic. To note his mind expanding under the light of knowledge, like a flower in the sun, was a spectacle most interesting to her, while before long the advantage became not wholly on one side, but reciprocal, and she found herself listening

almost as often to a tutor as talking to a
pupil. However simple were the views of
Tarilam they were original, and while as
natural as those of a child appealing to his
elders, were also as audacious. Untrammelled
by custom and the restrictions imposed by
education, he discussed with as much firmness
as freedom the ways of fate and the mysteries
of being. The simple but illogical faith of
his own people he had never accepted, but
had hitherto been content with a contempt-
uous tolerance of it. The theology which he
learned from Edith recommended itself to him
in many ways, but by no means exhausted his
spiritual curiosity. Aunt Sophia was often
not less appalled by the boldness of his specu-
lations than amazed by their intelligence.

On the other hand, there were reasons connected with Edith's antecedents—the blight
that had fallen upon her happiness in the loss
of her lover, and made a broken column of
her young life—that prevented these 'obsti-
nate questionings' from shocking her, and
even to some extent recommended the inter-
rogator. Not even in the old days, with

Layton himself, had she discussed these matters with so much freedom and interest.

After the employments of the day were over, some of which, too, he usually shared with the ladies, it was become a custom with the prince to join them at their evening meal; an officer or two, or the chaplain, would sometimes be of the party, and still more often Master Conolly, who would contribute to the amusements of the evening by his gift of song. But at other times Tarilam would visit the ladies quite alone, and on such occasions Edith found his company most agreeable, because he was then more like himself, and would express his natural sentiments without that dread of ridicule which had already found its place in a breast that had hitherto been absolutely fearless. One evening, when the three were occupied in the usual manner—the two ladies employed in needlework, and Tarilam fashioning some graceful ornament out of tortoiseshell, an art in which he was a proficient—their conversation was suddenly interrupted by a tumult without; there was a roar of voices and a rush of feet, and hardly had they risen from their chairs before the little cottage was surrounded by a mob of sailors and the parlour windows, which, as usual, were wide open, filled by excited and furious faces.

"What is the matter?" inquired Edith with quiet distinctness. Her face was pale, but otherwise she exhibited no sign of fear. Aunt Sophia, on the other hand, was speechless with terror. It was the impression of both women that a mutiny had broken out.

"Matter enough, miss," returned a voice she knew; it was that of William Dean, the gunner, a man who had always borne a good character, and behaved himself to her with great respect. "Murder's the matter, and yonder stands the man who did it."

He pointed to the prince, and as he did so a tumultuous and inarticulate cry of fury arose from those about him.

"Kill him! kill the nigger!"

"Make way then," interposed a brutal voice. "Don't talk, but do. Let me get a shot at him." And flushed with rage and liquor, the man Mellor, pistol in hand, here forced himself to the front, and levelled his weapon at Tarilam's head.

Before he could pull the trigger Edith had stepped swiftly between them.

"You vile coward," she cried. "Is there no man here who will see fair play and justice done?"

"Justice! Yes; we'll see justice done," answered a shrill voice. "Let us take him to the same spot, lads, where he killed the mate, and serve him likewise."

"What, without trial?" cried Edith vehemently. "Are you savages, then, who have forgotten that you were once Englishmen? William Dean, Luke Norman, Robert Ray, as you are honest men, I charge you to stand by me!"

"We mean no harm to *you*, miss," returned the gunner, "but as for this here prince, as he calls himself, we must have life for life."

"And so you shall, if he has taken life. I'll stake my own that he is innocent. Look at him, men, and tell me if he wears a murderer's face."

Like a curtain that conceals some noble

picture, she drew herself aside and showed him to them.

Motionless as a statue he stood confronting them, with a sort of mild amazement in his face. The confusion of tongues had prevented his half-cultured ear from catching what was said, but he could perceive that the intruders were violently enraged and against himself. It was his first experience (save one) of brutal passion in his new acquaintances, and it seemed to afford him all the interest of novelty. His eyes glanced from one to the other in dumb surprise, and then turned interrogatively to Edith.

" Tarilam does not understand," he murmured, with a quiet smile.

" They say you have committed a murder."

" No." Never was charge so serious met by so phlegmatic a denial. There was no more waste of tone than of words about it. If he had been accused of leaving the door open, he could not have defended himself with greater indifference, or at the same time more convincingly. The shake of the head that accompanied the monosyllable intensified alike

its force and its *sang froid.* " If anything of
the kind has happened," it seemed to say, " I
do assure you it was not I that did it."

Had his audience, indeed, been one capable
of appreciating the value of evidence, the
prince would have no longer been in danger;
but the men were blind with passion, and,
moreover, there were some among them less
concerned to detect a culprit than to sacrifice
a victim.

" He is lying! Kill the nigger! kill him,"
arose again from all sides; nor was it possible
that a catastrophe could have been much
longer averted had not a murmur from the
fringe of the crowd announced the arrival of
assistance. " Stand back, boys, here's the
captain!"

It was not indeed the captain, but his avant
courier, Master Conolly, who had run on
ahead of him, and with drawn cutlass was
in a moment scattering the crowd to left and
right. The man Mellor, indeed, presented his
pistol at him, but another sailor who stood
by struck the barrel upwards and the weapon
exploded in the air.

The sound of it seemed to remind the rest of the seriousness of their course of conduct and had a sobering effect, which was greatly increased by the appearance of the captain, followed by Mr. Redmayne, both armed to the teeth.

"Who fired that pistol?" he inquired, in a tone sharp and short as the shot itself.

"John Mellor."

"Is any one hurt here?" The captain was looking into the little parlour and 'counting heads' as he put the question.

"No, sir."

"That's well, and especially well for John Mellor," was the grim reply, "for if one hair of these ladies, or of the prince, their guest, had been injured, I would have shot him dead."

Mr. Mellor vanished silently away, and the crowd began to thin.

"You mutinous scoundrels!" continued the captain. "What is it you want that you must needs raise this tumult and disgrace yourselves in the eyes of our friend and ally?"

A murmur of discontent and menace ran through the crowd.

" He has committed murder."

" What, the prince ? Who says so ? Let the man that can prove it stand forth. Would you commit murder yourselves by slaying a man without trial ? That a foul crime has been done in our midst is only too true, but it cannot be wiped out by another. Come, all of you, to the officers' tent, and hear the matter sifted. Prince Tarilam, I must trouble you to come with us ; for though no assurance of yours is necessary to clear you in my eyes, this miserable suspicion must be stamped out."

With a pained and wondering look, such as children wear who are witnesses to the quarrels of their seniors, Tarilam bowed assent. It had been brought home to him for the first time that these superior people, dowered with such gifts and attributes that had seemed to him little short of superhuman, could be as violent and irrational, when the humour seized them, as the natives of Amrac. As he took leave of the ladies he retained Edith's hand in his for a few seconds.

"You stood between me and the short gun," he murmured with intense emotion. "But for you Tarilam would have been a dead man. He will never forget it."

"I ran no risk," she would have answered, but with his usual swift and noiseless tread he was gone in a moment.

Conolly and a couple of sailors who could be relied on were left behind as a guard for the ladies.

What had happened they had yet to learn, but that such a precaution should have been deemed necessary to their safety was full of sombre significance.

CHAPTER XV.

THE EXAMINATION.

THE 'officers' quarters' in the camp at
Faybur was a long narrow tent, furnished,
not uncomfortably, with the contents of half-
a-dozen cabins. Everything, however, had
this evening been moved away from the centre
of the apartment, to make room for a certain
something, which lay under a sheet on trestles,
and at once, with a terrible fascination, at-
tracted every eye. The feet standing out
stark and stiff, and the veiled face showing
sharply through its covering, presented the
unmistakable lineaments of death. How is it,
one wonders, that no sooner has the breath
of life departed than the very form that
contained it becomes new and strange to the
eyes of the living! Heaven forbid that it

O 2

may be no foretaste or analogue of the final separation from us of the soul.

Young as he was, Tarilam had seen death in many forms, nor had it for him the awe and mystery that it possesses for more cultured minds ; but as he followed the captain's steps, he approached the silent shape with a certain air of reverence as well as interest that had its effect upon the beholders. Quietly and without crowding, the majority of the cast-aways had entered the tent and were regarding his demeanour with keen attention. If the prince had really committed the murder, as one observed to the other, it could not have been the first by many, or he could scarcely have "kept himself so cool" in the presence of his victim. Once only he showed signs of perturbation, when they reached the corpse, and the captain gently drew back the sheet and revealed the features of the first mate. Then Tarilam uttered the dead man's name, with infinite gentleness, and sighed pro-foundly. "I did not know it had been so good a friend of mine," he simply said.

"So good a friend of all of us," exclaimed

the captain, vehemently. "A more dutiful officer and a more loyal messmate than Robert Marston never drew breath. My curse upon the cowardly hand that slew him."

"And mine," "And mine," cried several voices.

There was something menacing—nay, almost bloodthirsty—in the ring of them, which seemed to remind the captain that there was less need to arouse the general indignation than to turn it into the proper channel. When he spoke again his voice took a graver and more judicial tone. "This poor fellow here, my friends, was as dear to me as to any one of you, and none can be more resolved than I to avenge him; but, above all things, let us be just. We have no lawyers amongst us, but it will be possible, I hope, to get to the bottom of this matter without them; and, in the first place, it behoves us to hear what those have to say who saw him first where he lay dead. As for me, I know nothing except from hearsay. Mr. Redmayne yonder brings me word that Mr. Marston has been picked up on the beach with his head battered in, and Mr. Doyle reports that he is dead. That is all that I know for certain, and all that nine-tenths of you can know, yet I find fifty men have taken upon themselves to lay the guilt at the door of a fellow-creature because his skin is a trifle darker than their own. William Dean, you were one of those men. Now let us hear what accusation you bring against Prince Tarilam, and on what grounds."

The gunner stepped forward with an embarrassed air. "I know nothing, sir, but what I was told by my mates; they said that the prince had done it to their certain knowledge."

"*Who* said?" interrupted the captain, curtly; "let us have their names, if you please."

"Well, sir, there was Mellor for one."

"Very good, let Mellor stand forth. You are the man who fired a pistol just now at Mr. Conolly, to prove your detestation of murder, I suppose. Well, what do you know about this other?"

"The pistol went off of its own head in my

hand," growled Mellor. "I never meant to hurt the young gentleman; it was that prince as we were after."

"Why, what had he done?"

"Chucked Mr. Marston over the cliff."

The sort of murmur which is called 'sensation,' mixed with a note of assent, here arose from the crowd. They had found a spokesman to justify their late proceedings at last.

"You saw him do it, did you?"

"No, I didn't, but Rudge and Murdoch, they saw him."

"Let Rudge and Murdoch stand forth."

The two men obeyed, Rudge willingly and even demonstratively enough, Murdoch with less promptness. His face was white to the lips, and he kept it studiously averted from the spot where the dead man was lying.

"Now tell us what you know, Rudge."

"It was my afternoon off duty, and I was rambling about the island with Murdoch, and presently I got tired, and sat down to have a smoke, and Murdoch he went further on. I had not been two minutes alone, when I heard him cry out, 'Rudge! Rudge!' and I jumped up and ran to him. He was standing on the cliff top, pointing down below ; and I looked down and saw the body on the beach. ' Burst my buttons,' says I, ' why, if it ain't Mr. Marston.'

" ' Yes,' he cries, ' some one has pitched him over the cliff ; ' and he was shaking his head and flapping his hands, and very much put out about it was Murdoch."

" But how did he know Mr. Marston had been pushed over the cliff ? " inquired the captain. " Why might he not have fallen over."

" I suppose he never thought of that," said Rudge stolidly.

" That was it ; I never thought of that," echoed Murdoch, replying to his mate's look of inquiry. His voice was hoarse and mechanical ; and when he had spoken his tongue flickered about his lips as though they were in need of moisture.

" Now I should have thought that had been the most likely supposition to come into any man's mind, unless it was already running on something else," observed the captain reflectively. " Mr. Marston yonder," here he leant his head sideways towards his dead friend exactly as he would have done had he been alive, " was not one to make enemies."

" True for you, sir, that is so," was murmured on all sides.

" Then why should the notion of any one's having done him a mischief have entered into your mind ?" inquired the captain.

" The ground was trodden all about as though a struggle had been going on," exclaimed Rudge, " and the grass on the brink of the hill cliff was torn away in tufts as though some one had clung there till he had been flung off."

" I am speaking to Murdoch, not to you, Rudge," exclaimed the captain sharply. " I suppose he has a tongue of his own in his head like the rest of us."

If that was so, the person in question did not seem at all inclined to use it ; he stood silent, with his arms folded on his chest, his head sunk forward, and his eyes doggedly fixed upon the ground. The captain glanced from this unattractive object to his guest, who, with

head erect and fine form drawn to its full
height, presented indeed a strange contrast to
it. "Now I want to know who it was that,
having satisfied himself so easily that there
was murder done here, went a step further,
and laid it at the door of Prince Tarilam ? "

" It was Mr. Bates, sir," said the
gunner.

" Mr. Bates," exclaimed the captain, in
astonishment. "Then why is not Mr. Bates
himself here to say so ? "

" He ain't very well, sir," observed Rudge ;
"he was took bad at the sight of Mr. Marston.
But he told us with his own lips that the
prince had done it, for he had almost served
him the same trick himself, at the very same
place, not three weeks ago."

" Do you mean that he said the prince had
tried to throw *him* over the cliff ? "

" Yes, sir, he did, and that Mr. Conolly
caught him at it."

" Fetch Mr. Bates and Mr. Conolly here
this moment."

" Mr. Bates is ill in bed, sir."

" Then bring him out of his bed.   I don't

move from this spot till this affair is sifted to the very bottom."

As a legal investigation, the captain's method of proceeding left much to be desired. It was as haphazard and inconsequent as it was informal; but it was not altogether unadapted to the materials with which he had to deal; while the personal interest, and even the bias, he showed in the matter were far from being resented by his audience. The appearance of Matthew Murdoch, and the manner in which he had made his statement, had prejudiced them against him ; but they were also prejudiced against Tarilam. There was so little logic in their mental composition that they did not understand that if one of the two 'suspects' was guilty the other must needs be innocent.

Presently Mr. Bates appeared, led between two men, which gave him the air of being in custody. His face was red and swollen, his eyes were unnaturally prominent and wandered round the tent as if in search of something. When they lit upon the dead man, however, he took no more notice of him than if he had been asleep.

"It was Tarilam as did it," were his first words.

The captain, without attention to the abrupt and voluntary character of this statement, merely inquired, "How do you know that?"

"Because he tried to kill me in the same way. He held me over the cliff top and would have dropped me, just as he dropped Mr. Marston, and on the very same point of rock. He knew the best place to do it."

A murmur of indignation went round the tent. Here was evidence enough, indeed, and to the taste of the hearers.

The captain turned mechanically to the prince, who gravely bowed his head. "It is quite true that I meant to drop him," he quietly said. "He struck me."

There was a low growl of anger and discontent. "He has confessed it!" muttered a voice or two; and one man cried, "Hang him! hang him!"

The captain held up his hand for silence.

"Why was I never told of this, Mr. Bates?"

"Mr. Conolly asked me not to tell."

"Let us hear what Mr. Conolly has to say about it."

The midshipman had by this time arrived, followed by the two ladies, for whom the crowd made way. They did not, however, push to the front, but shrank from the neighbourhood of the dead body ; they had only just learnt the nature of the catastrophe which had caused the mob to invade their dwelling ; their distress on Mr. Marston's account was extreme, the elder lady was almost overwhelmed by it, and would willingly have remained within doors, but she could not permit her niece to come unattended, and Edith's interest in the living had overborne her natural tremors.

Conolly stepped forward and briefly stated what he knew of the rencontre between the prince and the third mate. It was quite true, he said, that he had kept silence upon the matter, but not more for the prince's sake than for that of Mr. Bates, who had committed an unprovoked assault upon him. The prince had resented it, no doubt, with unnecessary violence, but from what he (Conolly) knew of him, he was, he was persuaded, quite incapable of any such unprovoked and murderous outrage as was now laid to his charge.

The third mate seemed to take no notice of this observation; he moved his hands across his eyes, as though to sweep away some obstacle, and peered through the crowd in the direction of the ladies with anxious persistence.   Edith was speaking eagerly, though in low tones, to Mr. Redmayne, who, in his turn, whispered a few words to the captain.   " By all means.   Let us hear what Mr. Doyle has to say upon the matter," answered the latter aloud.

The surgeon, who had just removed from the captain's side to that of Mr. Bates, here answered to his name.

" When was it that you first saw Mr. Marston at the foot of the cliff ? "

" About an hour and a half ago, sir."

" Was he then alive ? "

" No, sir.   No man could have lived for one minute after such injuries as he had received.   On the other hand, from the condition of the body he could not have been dead long.   Half-an-hour at the most."

"You are confident of that," said the captain.

"I am quite certain that he had not been dead an hour."

"Miss Norbury," said the captain, "can you state with accuracy at what time Prince Tarilam came to your house this evening?"

Aunt Sophia strove to speak, but the situation was overpowering; the knowledge that every eye was turned on her, but especially the spectacle of the dead man, who seemed to be awaiting, like the rest, in dumb expectancy, her momentous reply, was too much for her nerves. "I can answer that question," said Edith, in a firm and confident tone, "for it so happened that I remarked to my aunt upon the circumstance that Prince Tarilam had joined us earlier than usual It was fully two hours ago."

"Did you look at your watch?"

"My aunt did so."

Here Aunt Sophia found her voice.

"It is quite true, Captain Head; it is exactly two hours and a half since the prince joined us."

A murmur of satisfaction ran through the crowd. The watch that Miss Norbury held in her hand appealed to their senses as no mere verbal testimony would have done.

" That circumstance, at all events, frees our guest from all suspicion of guilt in this matter," observed the captain. " I think it is due to him, Mr. Bates, that you should acknowledge as much."

The third mate answered not a word. He was staring wildly at Edith with both his hands stretched out before him. " I never pushed him over," he cried. " He jumped over of himself. I can't help his dripping with water. Keep him off, I say ; keep him off ! " The intense terror of the man manifest in his face and eye and trembling limbs was shocking to witness, and communicated itself to those about him. They fled from him in all directions, and left him standing by the corpse. The surgeon only kept his place by his side.

" Can any one explain the meaning of this ? " inquired the captain in an awe-struck tone. " Is it possible that this unhappy man is confessing to having perpetrated the crime himself?"

"No, sir," said Mr. Doyle, with an air of conviction. "It is fair to say that there is evidence enough that he was absent when the murder—for a murder I fear it was—was committed. Mr. Bates is suffering from an attack of delirium tremens."

CHAPTER XVI.

WAS IT POSSIBLE ?

SHOCKING as was the murder of Mr. Marston to his friend, the captain, it was hardly more terrible or symptomatic of trouble to come than was the professional dictum pronounced by Mr. Doyle as respected the third mate. Delirium tremens is not a disease that is engendered by occasional excess, though even that would make the circumstance of the gravest significance, but by long and continuous drinking habits ; and these had been proved to exist in one of his own officers, a man in duty bound to set an example of sobriety, and especially to discover and expose the drunkenness which had so mysteriously crept into the camp. That the offence was closely connected with the assassination of the first mate there could now be little doubt. Mr.

Marston had been very active in his endeavours to find out from whence the liquor came, and who supplied it, which had of late been demoralizing the men; and it was only too probable that in some solitary expedition he had come upon the delinquents in the very act of distillation, and had fallen a victim to their violence. Edith herself, as we know, had been stopped and turned back for a similar reason; and Tarilam had been treated in the like manner.

In their case their object had not been detection, and therefore their lives had not been sacrificed by those they had involuntarily disturbed in their wrong-doing. Mr. Marston, an officer devoted to his duties and to be deterred by no menaces of personal violence, had perished at their lawless hands. So far the matter was clear, but as to who had been the actual murderers—for it was probable, unless the first mate had been taken at a disadvantage, which the signs of conflict about the fatal place seemed to evidence, there were more than one—it was by no means certain.

P 2

Appearances seemed to point to Murdoch and Rudge, but not more strongly than to Mr. Bates himself, who, however, was freed from the consequence of his own confession (or what had looked very like it) by the testimony of Mr. Doyle, in whose company he had walked from the camp when the surgeon was summoned to the scene of the murder. At that time the third mate was sober enough, and had appeared greatly moved at what had happened. Indeed, it was Mr. Doyle's impression that Bates had taken to liquor immediately on his return to camp in order to drown the remembrance of the spectacle he had just beheld.

For the present, such were the doubts and difficulties that overhung the case, the murderer of Mr. Marston remained unpunished, a thing itself of sombre import and evil augury. Mr. Bates, indeed, was deprived of his rank, and solemnly warned that on the next occasion of being found in a state of intoxication he should be soundly flogged; but even this measure, however just and salutary, had danger in it, since it openly threw into the arms of the disaffected an ally to whom there still clung some relics of authority.

If, then, circumstances gave rise to apprehension in a man so solid and "four-square to every wind that blew" as Captain Head, we may imagine how they affected the ladies. It was only too evident to them that Faybur had ceased to be that paradise in which, though cut off from home and friends, they had long resigned themselves to pass their lives. To Edith, indeed, the prospect had been even welcome, but neither Aunt Sophia or herself had contemplated the possibility of such events as had lately taken place. The place was an Eden still, but not the same Eden to them as it had been before the serpent had made known its presence. The stain of murder seemed to blotch the fairness of Nature herself; the fumes of liquor to mingle with the perfumes of the air ; and the dark clouds of insecurity to gather shape and volume in the azure sky. Only one or two were in all probability connected with the actual crime, but it was only too likely that others were cognizant of it, and it was no wonder that a certain distrust of their own people arose in the two women's minds. This was greatly intensified by the late behaviour of the sailors towards the prince; Edith especially could not forget the spectacle of those furious faces at her window, or the cries with which they had demanded his innocent blood. They would have taken the life of the man to whom she owed her own, not only without scruple, but with eager and tumultuous joy. When she contrasted their bloodthirsty demeanour with the noble calm with which her guest had confronted it, the question, "Which was the savage?" could hardly fail to occur to her; and it could have but one reply.

The prince's behaviour in the tent had impressed her still more favourably. Some of the proceedings had necessarily been unintelligible to him, but he knew at least that the result of them would be a matter of life or death to him; this, indeed, had been clear even to his two attendants, who directly he made his appearance had loyally pressed forward to protect his person.

"Commit no violence," he had said to them

in his own language. "Whatever happens to me, if I am killed, tell the king, my father, not to avenge my death." And from that moment he had remained unmoved, like one who, though on the verge of the grave, has nothing to trouble him, his final dispositions having been made.

Edith, who had learnt from him sufficient of the Bredan tongue to understand what he had said, asked him the reason of it, since it was hardly to be expected that her efforts in the direction of religious culture could have taught him the sublime lesson of forgiveness of injuries.

" I told my father not to avenge my death," he said, " because I felt that if I was condemned to die, it would be done under a mistake." The explanation, though highly creditable, appeared, considering the simplicity of the speaker, a little subtle ; there was, moreover, an expression in his face that was new to her ; for it conveyed for the first time the idea of concealment.

" Was that your only reason ? " she inquired.

" No," was the quiet reply ; " I did not want war to occur on my account, since if it did so, it would set your people's faces against you, because you had been Tarilam's friend."

"That was very good and thoughtful of you," said Edith, with gentle gravity and a blush, which she strove in vain to repress.

Tarilam raised his eyebrows; the precautions he had taken for her safety had occurred to him so naturally that he was wholly unconscious of their chivalry.

"When things seemed going against you, prince, and the horrid men were shouting that you were guilty," said Aunt Sophia a little afterwards—she was curious about the young man's 'views,' and given to sounding him when she got him alone—" did you feel no fear?"

He smiled and shook his head disdainfully.

" But there would be nothing to be ashamed of if you did," she persisted; " death has its terrors even for Christian folk."

He opened his large eyes in wonder.

" When we die in Breda," he said, "there is no more trouble; the Amrac people cannot reach us. The storm may rage upon the water, but it does not wake us; we sleep in peace."

" But you would have been taken away

from those who are dear to you—your father, for example."

"It would not be for long; my father is old, and would soon rejoin me."

"And Majuba ?"

"Majuba would grieve," he admitted gravely.

"And would not Edith grieve also, don't you think ?"

"Would it be worth her while ? Who is Tarilam ?"

"It was worth her while to risk her life for him when the sailor would have shot him," said Miss Norbury reproachfully.

"Do you suppose I do not remember ?" he answered plaintively. "I know a boy who had a tame sea-gull, that had broken its wing; it got down to the water, and would have been blown out to sea and died, had he not plunged in after it, though the bay was full of sharks. It was a generous instinct, but it was not worth while."

"But Edith likes you better than the boy his bird."

"Do you really think so ?" His eyes kindled with eager light.

" Why, of course. Did you not save her life ? "

" Ah, yes," he sighed. "It was because she remembered that." The light went out from his face ; his voice took a tone of hopeless despondency, the meaning of which it was impossible for any woman to mistake.

"My poor prince !" murmured Aunt Sophia to herself sympathetically.

Though a match-maker to the core, she shrank from having any hand in such an affair as this; she was not particular about the eligibility of a *parti*, provided that he was ' nice ' in himself, and would be likely to make a good husband. If everything else had promised well, she might even have been inclined to forgive a difference of race in a European, but the notion of an inhabitant of Breda, however princely and attractive, however chivalrous and unselfish, venturing to lift his eyes to Edith was a shock to her. She liked the prince, but it was out of the question that she could give him any assistance as a suitor, even if such help could have availed him, which she felt confident it could not. A girl that had loved Charles Layton would never listen to poor Tarilam; she did not say, even to herself, would never stoop to listen, for she was not without appreciation of his noble qualities; but the unlikeness of the two men was too pronounced to admit of her picturing the possibility of the one being substituted for the other.

She did not understand that so far as that difference affected the matter at all, it weighed with Edith in Tarilam's favour. If there had been anything in him to remind her of her former lover in the faintest degree, she would not have admitted him to her intimacy. As it was, it never struck her that in so doing she was giving him a certain encouragement. He could never have found the pathway to her heart which Layton had trodden; every step would have disinterred some dead regret; but was it not possible that he might reach it by some road of his own? He was like some untutored mathematical genius who attempts a problem in the schools by a method worked out by himself, less direct and less convenient, indeed, than the authorized one, but which, nevertheless, solves it.

The consciousness of having done her best for him in the late fracas no doubt strengthened Edith's interest in the young fellow; for if we are inclined to hate those we have injured, it is no less true that those we have benefited thereby establish a claim upon our affections. And yet if it had been suggested to Edith Norbury that she had even begun to entertain a tender passion for Prince Tarilam, she would have denied the imputation with indignation, though not with the contempt which the idea had aroused in Aunt Sophia.

CHAPTER XVII

AFTER the social storm which had threatened such damage to the little community of castaways, there ensued a calm in Faybur. The murder of Mr. Marston, though its perpetrators remained undiscovered, produced a very deep effect; and while it shocked the majority, very literally sobered the malcontents. In the latter case, perhaps the fear of discovery induced good behaviour in the most of them, but, at all events, there was no further outbreak, either of drunkenness or insubordination.

The continuance of bad weather still prevented the other natives of Breda from visiting the island, but the two that had accompanied the prince had made themselves so pleasant and so useful as to afford the most lively

hopes of concord between their fellow-countrymen and the ship's company. As to Tarilam
himself, the falseness of the accusation against
him having once been admitted, public feeling
veered round in his favour, and his gentle
and genial qualities being thus afforded a fair
chance of appreciation, he became extremely
popular. A few only held aloof from him ;
the degraded mate and his three myrmidons,
Mellor, Rudge, and Murdoch.

"If the prince comes to harm through any
act of your friends," the captain had informed
Mr. Bates, with a vigour of language which
modern type would be at a loss to reproduce,
"and I fail for the second time in bringing
the murder home to any one of you, as sure
as my name is Henry Head I'll hang you all
four"—a warning that had the happiest effect
in putting all notion of pistolling the prince
out of their minds; as to attacking him without firearms, and in no greater disproportion
of force than four to one, they had not so
much as entertained the idea of it. Mr.
Bates never saw Tarilam without a certain
swimming of the head, produced by the re-

collection of being held at arm's length over
the precipice where a far worthier life than
his own had found its end; and the narrative
of that experience, told with much personal
feeling, if without dramatic artifice, had had
a most wholesome effect upon his three
friends.

From the sentimental, or Paul-and-Virginia
point of view, the attractions of such an island
as Faybur were manifest. It was quite the
place for two young lovers to dwell in, "the
world forgetting, by the world forgot," till
they both died together on the same day in
one another's arms; but it did not afford
scope enough for the energies of upwards of
a hundred British sailors. There was not
enough work for them to do, and too little
room for play. They took but limited interest
in literature, chiefly from the fact that only a
very few of them could read. Under Edith's
auspices, Tarilam indeed had become a better
scholar than almost any of them except the
officers. No one wrote but the captain, who
kept a journal which he called a log, and
which was wooden enough to merit its title.

Conversation languished in the tents for want of a topic.

Under these circumstances it was only natural that since a murdered man, whose assassin had never been discovered, was buried in the place, that his ghost should occasionally be seen. Ghosts are not seen in large towns, but in country places, where monotony and some poor substitute for imagination beget them. With the trifling exception of the *Phantom Ship*, which has something professional about it to excuse its appearance, ghosts are only seen at sea under the most appropriate circumstances, *i. e.* in a dead calm. Captain Head felt it to be a bad sign that poor Mr. Marston did not rest in the grave which had been dug for him in the most beautiful spot in the whole island, but must needs walk all over it, and meet the very last men in the ship's company whom he would have chosen to consort with during life. Mellor and Rudge had both seen him, and had had fits in consequence. It was whispered that Murdoch was in the constant habit of seeing him, though he was very reticent upon

the matter himself, and that Mr. Bates remained in his tent, as obstinately as Achilles,
after nightfall, for fear of being addressed by
his quondam brother officer, albeit, when in
the flesh they had not been on speaking terms.
If the vision had been confined to these
scoundrels, they might have been welcome to
it, but others had seen it, or thought they
had seen it, and the whole morale of the camp
was getting endangered by the superstition.
The captain, who suspected trick, rather en-
couraged testimony in order that he might
get to the root of the matter. One evening
William Dean asked for a few words in private
with him.

The gunner was known to be a good fellow,
though he had been carried away by the late
whirlwind of indignation aroused by Bates
against the prince, and was by no means
a liar — indeed he had not the imagination for it. "Cap'n," he said, very gravely
and respectfully, "I've seen somethink just
now."

"Very good; I am glad you came to tell
me at once," was the sardonic reply; "one

likes to have the very latest information from the spirit world."

"But I am not sure as he *was* a spirit."

"Oh, this is a new phase.   Mr. Marston has come to life again has he?"

"It was not Mr. Marston, cap'n.   It was the Malay."

"What do you mean?   The man that came over with the Bredan folk?"

"Yes, sir."

"But they can't come over in this weather?"

"Nevertheless, not half-an-hour ago, I saw him as sure as my name is William Dean."

"Where?"

"Not fifty yards from the look-out.   He seemed to be coming away from it, though that could hardly be, as the man on duty saw nothing of him."

"Who *is* the man on duty?"

"Matthew Murdoch."

The captain's face became very grave. "Now just say how it happened."

"Well, I thought I would climb up the cliff to have a pipe and see how the wind lay; it was falling a bit, and the sea going down all round, they told me. When I was within twenty feet of the top, or so, there stood a man by himself, who was looking right down into the camp. He kept himself behind a bush, but I saw him before he saw me, and he was not a white man."

" Why should he not have been one of the prince's men ?"

" Because I had left them both below. Moreover, he had only a waistcloth, such as the Malay wore. The sight of him upset me, and I stumbled ; the noise made him glance towards me, and our eyes met, and the Malay it was, sure enough. He was off like a bird, and into the bush in a moment."

" Did you run after him ?"

" No ; I knew it was no good. I went on to the flagstaff ; Murdoch had his back to me, but heard me coming. ' They are quiet enough down there, I suppose,' he said."

" What did he mean by that ?"

" Well, I guess he thought I was somebody else."

The captain took in all the possibilities at a glance. A spy on the island, and Murdoch

Q 2

in traitorous communication with him—ambush and massacre! "And when he found out it was you?"

"He started a bit; then, says I, 'I have seen the Malay.' 'What Malay?' he asks, as quiet as could be, and swore nobody had been near him since he had come on the watch."

"And what do *you* think about it, William Dean?"

"As far as the Malay is concerned, sir, I *don't* think about it; I am sure of it. As to the other, I don't wish to get any man into trouble, though Murdoch's no mate of mine."

"Quite right. You can keep a still tongue in your head, I know. Now, say not a word to anybody, but send the first mate here at once."

Mr. Redmayne was now first mate in Mr. Marston's room, the vacancy caused by Bates's degradation having been filled up by Arthur White, the midshipman. He was but a young hand for such a place, and indeed there was no one now save Mr. Redmayne and the surgeon on whose authority and judgment the captain could rely.

Within ten minutes Mr. Redmayne had started, with eight men armed to the teeth, to make the circuit of the island to search for canoes.

If the Malay was really in Faybur, he must have come by boat, in spite of the heavy weather. Such light vessels as were used in Breda could of course be carried up from the shore and hidden in the bush, but hardly, unless carried by many hands, without leaving some sign of their passage on the sand. To search the island itself before daylight was useless.

A little before midnight the party returned without result. No canoe had been discovered, but at the north end of the island, opposite Breda, there were indentations in the sand which some thought had been caused by the hauling up of a canoe, and others not. They were very indistinct, and the question was whether they had been rendered so by design, or whether the marks were solely accidental. The next day the whole island was thoroughly investigated by scouting parties, who came upon the distilling apparatus which had been the cause of so much evil, and destroyed it; in view of which achievement the expedition could hardly be said to have been labour in vain; but no trace of any alien visitor was discovered. Upon the whole, the captain was inclined to think that William Dean's Malay was made of the same material as furnished for others Mr. Marston's ghost; but, like a wise man whose motto is "No risk," he caused the night rounds to be more frequent, practised beating to quarters to such perfection that every man was at his post in a few seconds, and enacted that two men instead of one should always keep watch at the look-out.

A few days after these arrangements had been made, Mr. Redmayne and Mr. White had the good luck to come upon what would at a sea-side place at home have made the fortune of the locality; a bay of shells, or rather a bay of sand beneath which lay such a treasure of shells as only a child's imagination could have pictured. They were of all sizes, some of them reaching to such proportions that a single one would in our English gardens have sufficed for a grotto, and of the most

splendid colours. In hue, indeed, they resembled nothing so much as those gorgeous
sea anemones which line, as with precious
stones, the Gouliot caves in Sark; or those
too brilliant mushrooms which a benevolent
society has painted for us in colours and
labelled 'edible,' without finding a human
being with the courage to touch them.

The two discoverers, though by no means
given to 'gush' over the wonders of nature,
were carried by the spectacle into unaccustomed regions of speculation.   " How strange,
it seems," observed the newly-promoted
middy, " that things so marvellously beautiful,
and so fitted to delight the eye, should be
covered with sand!"

" Depend upon it, everything is ordained
for the best," returned Mr. Redmayne gravely.
" Think what a pleasure it will be to Miss
Edith to discover them for herself! At the
same time I wish—while Nature was about it
—that the bay had been placed a little nearer
to the camp."

It was, in fact, almost at the northern
extremity of the island, at the very place

where Edith had met with such rough treatment from the distillers, where the cliffs were
the most sheer and the vegetation most
luxuriant. It was nothing of a walk, however,
to one like herself, in the highest state of
vigour, to which, thanks to the exhilarating
climate and her wholesome mode of life, one
of her sex could attain, and the attractions of
the place, as Mr. Redmayne had foreseen,
were overpowering to her. He himself had
piloted her to the spot, where her pleasure at
the spectacle gave him ten times the enjoyment he had experienced when beholding it
for the first time, but she was never weary of
visiting it, no matter who were her companions. When it was possible, however, Mr.
Redmayne always made one of her escort, a
privilege to which, under the circumstances,
he thought he had a reasonable claim. The
expedition was rather beyond Aunt Sophia's
pedestrian powers, and she contented herself
with gloating over the shelly treasures her
niece brought home with her in such profusion
that their little home soon resembled some
haunt of the mermaids.

One morning Edith started for 'Shell Bay,' as it was called, as usual accompanied by the prince and the first mate. On their last visit a strange bird of uncommon size had been seen hovering over the spot, and Mr. Redmayne had therefore provided himself with a musket, peace having so long reigned at Faybur that the edict against the waste of gunpowder was in some degree relaxed. At the moment of their departure, however, his presence was required in connection with the storage of some dried provisions; while hardly had he hurried off, when a message from the captain, requiring the personal services of the prince in respect to the yam plantation, which had been established under his auspices, took away Edith's remaining escort.

As both her companions promised to rejoin her, however, directly the public service had been attended to, she saw no reason for postponing the pleasure she had promised herself. They could travel, of course, much faster than she could, and would probably overtake her before she reached the bay. The road took her by the look-out, where, as it happened, Murdoch and Mellor were on duty. They saluted her respectfully, but she returned the civility with coldness and very hurriedly; she distrusted both the men, and had a firm conviction that the guilt of Mr. Marston's murder lay at Murdoch's door. The sight of him was hateful to her, and dashed her spirits, though it was so far satisfactory to know that his duties for the day would prevent him from coming across her on her proposed expedition. Hardly had she passed them, when one of them cried out to the other; she looked back and saw the flag descending the staff—a piece of carelessness in him who had charge of it which might well have aroused the reproof of his companion. Nevertheless, she noticed on surmounting the next hill—where she stood still a moment to rest herself—that the flag still remained half-mast high, as though the halyards had got twisted.

CHAPTER XVIII.

THE BLOW-PIPE.

THE day was a most lovely one even for Faybur, and the sea, which had recently been of milder mood, was showing even more pronounced signs of calm. In a few days at farthest there would be arrivals from Breda; the coming of the king had little interest for her, but she looked forward with some excitement to the visit from Majuba which Tarilam had promised her, so soon as the fine weather should set in. She had a great curiosity, mixed with a certain apprehension, to see what Majuba was like. "I hope," Aunt Sophia had said in her simple way, "that she will not be tattoed everywhere, or have feathers in her hair."

This was not very likely, but it was not impossible, and Edith felt that any trace of savagery in Tarilam's sister would be a shock to her. She was thinking of this and of matters generally connected with her present life, in a manner which some months ago would have seemed impossible; the old life had not passed away from her, for now and again it returned to her with great force and distinctness of regret, but it had been marvellously superseded by the new. Though so much that had made up what we call home was wanting in it, Faybur had become in its way a home to her. This was a substitution less difficult to effect in her case than in another's, since what makes home most worthy of the name had long been unknown to her; the central figures round the hearth in place of father and mother had been those of her uncle and her cousin, of whom, dead and gone though they were, she could not trust herself to think, because they had been her Charley's enemies. Had any one near and dear to her remained in England—thus she reflected upon the matter without daring to say to herself "Had Charley been alive"—this transference of her home sympathies would have been impossible. But, in truth, she no longer looked upon this island with alien eyes. (It did, in fact, hold all she could be said to love; for though we love the dead, it is in another fashion.) Its incomparable scenes of beauty, while they still fascinated her, had grown familiar; her observation of nature had become extraordinarily acute, though it fell far short of that of Tarilam. She knew the trees by the music which the wind evoked from them, the flowers by their perfume, and even the herbs by the fragrance they emitted beneath her tread. The sea only was strange to her; it was not like that ocean of which she had had so bitter an experience; those unknown islands in the horizon gave it a certain mystery from which she shrank.

To-day they seemed nearer than usual, and Breda, of course, the nearest. She had no wish to visit it; the idea of so doing filled her with vague aversion, which the prince, having perceived, had henceforth forebore to speak about his home. It was curious that while he so willingly gave himself up to self-reflection, Edith avoided it; one of the reasons which had caused her to welcome so trifling a matter as the discovery of the shells was that it gave her occupation; she disliked being left, as now, to her own company and her own thoughts. If they reverted to the past, they distressed her; if they concerned themselves with the future, they were equally hopeless, though necessarily more indefinite. She preferred to live in the present, from day to day, without retrospection and without forecast; a state of emotion in direct contrast to that to which she had formerly been accustomed.

She was glad, therefore, since she had not been rejoined by either of her late companions, when she found herself at her journey's end. It was not much to do, but it was better than thinking, to disinter from their sandy beds these splendid shells, almost as valuable in a European mart as precious stones, and ten times more beautiful. Of their scientific names—if, indeed, they were known to science —she knew nothing, nor even the terms applied to their formation; she did not even know the difference between a crenated and

a dentated shell; but she was charmed by
their exquisite loveliness or their imperial
splendour. Some were diaphanous, and, being
held up to the light, disclosed secret chambers,
"pavilions of tender green"; others, though
opaque, resembled pyramids of glowing flame.
She was pushing away the sand from a specimen which struck her as being lovelier than
the rest, when suddenly she became aware
that she was not alone; two figures which
had suddenly emerged from the reef of rock
to northwards, were making towards her with
great speed.

In her extreme surprise she made no
attempt to escape, which, indeed, must have
been utterly futile, nor was she very much
alarmed, since from the look of the men she
took them at first for the prince's two attendants; but as they drew nearer she perceived
that, though dressed in similar attire, and
probably of the same race, they were not the
men she knew, and were armed with clubs.
With noiseless swiftness they ran up and
seized her arms, and each, placing a hand
behind her, began to impel her towards the

spot from which they came. She neither assisted their movements nor resisted them, but was borne along in silence; the whole transaction seemed to her a kind of hideous nightmare, in which she had no volition. As they rounded the reef, however, they came face to face with the Malay, whom she recognized, while beyond him, some quarter of a mile away, was a canoe drawn up on the sand. Then at once it flashed upon her that nothing less than her abduction was intended, and she uttered a bitter cry of distress and despair.

It was echoed, or so it seemed, from the top of the cliff, which in that furthermost bay was as sheer as the precipice where Mr. Marston had met his death, though somewhat more closely hung with creepers. Down this pathless steep was fluttering something winged and white, like a bird with a broken wing. She scarcely recognized it for what it was, so incredible did it appear that any human being should venture to descend that airy steep, yet something within her whispered " Tarilam." She had eyes for nothing save that terrible descent, which was apparently accomplished in safety. Still, against three men, two of them little inferior in stature to himself, what, though he had reached the bottom unharmed, could even his prowess effect? She felt that he was about to rush towards her, and, unarmed, precipitate himself upon her captors, two of whom carried clubs, and the Malay a long knife. Then he would be slain before her eyes, and the sacrifice of his priceless life would have been made in vain.

No sooner did he touch the ground, however, than he ran like an arrow, not toward herself, but in the direction of the canoe. A cry of alarm burst from the three men, who perceived his object more quickly than she did, and the Malay and one savage darted forward to prevent his carrying it into effect, while the other snatched up Edith in his brawny arms and followed after them at scarcely less speed. The canoe was much nearer to her captors than to Tarilam, and though his swiftness was such that he went three feet to their two, they reached it first. As they stooped to launch it, however, he was within a few yards of them, and, stooping suddenly, took up a huge stone. They dropped their burthen, and the Malay drew his knife from its sheath, and the savage a little instrument from his bosom—it was a blow-pipe.

Tarilam made a feint of throwing the stone at them, which caused them to jump aside from the canoe, at which he instantly aimed it. It struck the frail bark in the centre and shattered it to atoms.

Then he turned back and flew at the man who was carrying Edith. The savage put her down, but twisted his hand in her long hair, by which he grasped her firmly. He looked at the broken canoe and the coming foe and gnashed his teeth; all means of escape were cut off from him, and he read aright in the prince's eyes a sentence of immediate death. Something, however, was still left him—vengeance. He raised his club and was about to brain his defenceless and half-fainting captive, when a sharp report rang out from the cliff top, and a bullet crashed through his brain. He fell, and would have dragged Edith with

him but that Tarilam's arm was already
around her waist. She clung to him, but
he gently untwined her arms, and placed her
so that his form interposed itself as a shield
between her and a new danger. At the
report of the gun, which, it is needless to
say, had been thus opportunely fired by Mr.
Redmayne, the Malay had instantly dashed
across the sands into the woods; but the
remaining savage, while equally recognizing
that the fortune of war was against him, and
even doubtless crediting his enemies with
supernatural assistance, entertained no thought
either of flight or submission. A gesture of
astonishment at the noise and smoke of the
musket, and the fatal effect upon his comrade,
had been extorted from him for the moment,
but he had immediately recovered his presence
of mind, and with malignant deliberation was
advancing towards the prince and Edith with
his blow-pipe at his mouth. It seemed strange
that such a little toy should excite in so
dauntless a breast so intense an apprehension
as Tarilam now exhibited; not, indeed, on his
own account, since he so freely offered himself

as a mark for it, but no hen threatened by hawk ever exhibited a more passionate anxiety to protect her little ones than the prince now manifested to screen his charge. His nostrils dilated with terror, his bronzed face took a hue more near to pallor than would have seemed to be possible; he stood like one who sees hovering o'er his head the very angel of death, and listens perforce to the beating of her wings.

Once more the musket rang out from the cliff top, but this time without effect; it was fired from a lower elevation, but the marksman in the act of descending by a zigzag route, as quickly as the nature of the ground permitted, had not taken so true an aim; the savage half turned his head at the report, and on looking again towards his intended victims beheld Tarilam within ten feet of him, a flying incarnation of rage. The next moment both were on the ground, their hands on one another's throats, in a death grapple. It did not last long; Edith knew that it could not. She watched it with horror, but not so far as Tarilam was concerned with apprehension;

man to man a struggle with the prince she was well convinced could have but one ending. Presently he rose, leaving his adversary stretched motionless on the ground, and staggered towards her. She flew to meet him, and in her turn strove to support his tottering form. "Has he wounded you, my prince?" she cried, with passionate solicitude.

"No, dear, he has killed me," he answered with a smile. "Tarilam is swift, but not so swift as an Amrac arrow. The woorali poison is in my veins."

"Oh, Tarilam, dear Tarilam, what is to be done?" she cried despairingly. "There must be *some* thing. Think, think! what *can* I do for you?"

"Kiss me," he murmured with exquisite tenderness; "that is all I ask. Kiss me, Edie," and with that he fell fainting on the sand.

END OF VOL. II.

www.ingramcontent.com/pod-product-compliance
Lightning Source LLC
Chambersburg PA
CBHW030813020726

47499CB00006B/1889